WHERE'D YOU GO?

WHERE'D YOU GO?

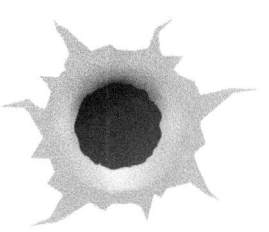

KEHINDE ADEMOYE

origami

Parrésia Publishers Ltd.
82, Allen Avenue, Ikeja, Lagos, Nigeria.
+2348154582178, +2348062392145
origami@parresia.com.ng
www.origami.com.ng

ISBN: 978-978-56595-2-8

Printed in Nigeria by Parrésia Press

To
Lieutenant Colonel Abu Ali,
Captain Oluwasola Akingbesote,
and all heroes who paid the ultimate sacrifice to insurgency
(Your labour will not be in vain)
and
Those still in the front
(Our prayers are with you)

"…Anger can at times be creative. One writes a great poem, a great symphony. One does something special for the sake of humanity, because one is angry at the injustice that one witnesses. But indifference is never creative."

– Elie Weisel

(The Perils of Indifference; April, 1999).

CONTENTS

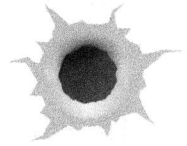

AMBUSHED

I

Captain Sholae and his company were going on patrol. They were serving around communities recently ravaged by insurgent herdsmen. Their commander, who they all called Colonel C.O behind his back, had given the orders for the patrol after the last skirmish with armed herdsmen in the sector.

The Captain got on his knees and said his prayers as he did every morning. 'Dear God, keep my men and me safe on our patrol today, as you have been doing. Keep my family safe. Restore peace to our nation, Nigeria. Amen.' After that, he called his men for prayers, a pep talk to boost their morale, and instructions for the march.

'Amen!' the men of Scorpion Company responded to the Muslim prayer; they responded with same fervour to the Christian invocation prayed in Jesus' name. Prayers were said for safety, peace and their loved ones.

The soldiers in Scorpion Company acted like a family. They talked honestly among themselves about their fears, their irritations and their loved ones. Once a week, Captain Sholae called the platoons together and listened to his men.

Two days before, some of the men had spoken about their losses. One soldier had lost loved ones in Benue; another reminisced about a dead half-sister in the skirmish in Plateau state. Two soldiers did not know the state of their father's houses and their maternal uncles in Lafia. Captain Sholae, flanked by his lieutenants, listened to his men's tales of pain.

The Captain told his men, 'I can't truly say I understand how you feel, but I know God will give us victory and all these…' he spread his hands around, 'will count for something.'

One of the men, a sergeant, spoke. 'Oga, amen. But it is not God who put us in this mess. It is human beings.' The men nodded and murmured their agreement.

'That is true, but we hope things will get better. That is why we are fighting. We are on the frontlines and must keep doing our part to bring safety and sanity to our people.'

'Sir, they send us to go and die for this country; yet the people accuse us of colluding with the enemy,' a lieutenant pointed out.

'Politicians play politics with our lives and then turn around and do propaganda with our deaths. Where do we go now, sir!' another soldier added.

Captain Sholae was silent. He knew the angst of his men, and he knew that one sometimes had to be quiet to empathise.

'You feefu ask why I deribe fleasure in killing those bastard terrorists?' It was Garba, a Lance Corporal who had lost all his family members to a Boko Haram attack in Madagali, in Adamawa state. He rarely ever spoke; when he did, his words dripped with anguish. 'Do you know what zey zid to my pamily. Danboroba, shege!' he spat.

Captain Sholae pacified his men and spoke to them in a clear, strong voice. 'We are not politicians; we are soldiers. Let us do our job and make this nation peaceful.'

'Oga, why do you believe so much in this country? Nobody cares about anybody, so why should we?'

Captain Sholae looked up. 'Nigeria is the only country we have. We have to make it better for our children and us. This is our home, and we must fight for its peace. Where ever we go, we will always be visitors. We have to fix our land; that is why we keep the faith.'

The soldiers looked at their Captain and smiled; something about his words increased their morale and bolstered their resolve.

One of the soldiers murmured, 'If only a patriot like this was in power.' If Captain Sholae heard the murmur, he did not show.

Captain Sholae mapped out the area the various platoons were to cover. He charged his lieutenants and asked them to rendezvous at 1600hrs.

The Captain noticed one of the men looked flushed and called him over.

'Corporal, are you okay?'

'Yes, sir. Good to go, sir.'

'You don't look too good to me.'

'Sir,' the soldier began, 'I am good…'

'Sit this one out.' Captain Sholae said, patting him on the shoulder. 'There will be other patrols.'

'Sir, I want to play my part. I am good to go, sir,' the soldier said, trying his best not to argue.

'You are already playing your part by being here; perhaps better than most. You left your family and put your country first. Sit this one out and get your strength back. I don't want to have to worry about you out there. I need everyone at a hundred percent.'

'Yes, sir.'

'Carry on,' Captain Sholae said. He put his helmet under his arm and made for his troops.

'Be safe out there, sir.'

'We will. That's the plan.'

II

The soldiers moved out and faced their designated areas. 'See you at 1600hrs. Remember, I want you to check in every hour, on the hour.' the Captain said before getting into the Humvee.

'Yes sir!'

'And boys,' the Captain called, 'Be safe out there.'

Captain Sholae went with one of the platoons. As they moved towards their area, his mind went to his family. He missed them very much; he had been quite emotional when he spoke with his wife and son the previous night. He was looking forward to going home in December so that he could spend Christmas with his family. He recalled the promise his wife had extracted from him: she made him swear to come back alive. He had told her that no one could determine who survived or died in battle. But she had insisted, and he had sworn. Now, he was glad he had kept his promise so far. In a few weeks, he would be holding his wife and son in his arms again by God's grace.

They parked their Humvees and proceeded on foot. Captain Sholae raised a fist, signalling his men to stop. He signalled his men to proceed through the footpath cautiously. When they got in the open, they moved in a staggered column formation toward the village ahead. The village looked deserted; no kids were playing or women going about. He could not see any men either. It was 1145hrs. Captain Sholae knew something was amiss.

'Be alert guys, something is not right with this location,' Captain Sholae said. He faced the officer close to him, 'Did the intelligence report say this village was deserted?'

'No, sir.'

'Keep your eyes open, boys. Something is not quite right.'

As they got to the entrance of the village, the other teams checked in. 'Alpha Team, this is Bravo Team checking in. It is all quiet in our location,' the officer gave their coordinates. Teams Charlie and Delta checked in too. All seemed well in their locations. The Captain told their radio man to give their coordinates and inform the others they might need reinforcement as the village they were entering had a strange vibe.

'Roger that sir, we can be in your position in five. Over.'

'Over and out.'

When the soldiers reached the first house, the scout got on one knee and scanned the area. Another soldier was behind him, on his feet, his gun on the ready. 'Clear!' The scout shouted and waved the other soldiers to advance.

The others joined them and they spread out, checking the area.

'Clear!'

'Clear!'

They were close to the village square when a little boy walked towards them with his football in his hands. The boy let the ball fall out of his hand; it rolled towards the Captain. The Captain smiled at the boy and kicked the ball back to him. The boy moved his head from side to side as he mouthed, 'Trap.'

The scout rushed towards the six-year-old looking boy but did not get to him early enough. A bullet tore through the boy.

'Ambush!' the Captain yelled as the scout caught a bullet in the chest. The soldiers scattered. The Captain shot in the direction he believed the bullets were coming from; he pulled the scout by the vest and dragged him to the side of the closest building while his men returned fire.

'Contact right!' yelled a soldier as he engaged the enemy along with some men.

'Contact left!' another soldier shouted.

'Multiple contacts!' the Captain yelled. They were surrounded.

The enemy came from all fronts with the soldiers repelling them. The radio man called for backup. 'Bravo, Charlie, Delta teams, come in. We have been ambushed. I repeat, we have been ambushed; we are taking heavy fire. Requesting immediate backup.' But the other teams were under attack too. The Captain asked the radioman to call the base. 'Scorpion team to base; Scorpion team to base. We are under attack and taking heavy fire; we need support now! I repeat we are under attack and taking serious fire. Requesting immediate backup!'

By the time the radio man made to give their coordinates, their attackers had jammed their signal.

The Captain faced his men. 'We need to make our stand here.

We might not make it out, but we'll show these bastards the strength of the Nigerian Army. The nation is greater than anybody. For God and for country!'

'For God and for country!' they echoed. 'Ahua!'

III

The scout was back on his feet and in the fight. His vest had saved him. The Captain noted they staying huddled up put them at a disadvantage. He saw a building close by and decided he needed to get some men there so they could fight the enemy from two fronts.

'Give me cover fire. I want to make for that building. I need four men with me.'

'Sir, this move is dangerous. We need you here,' stated a Sergeant, 'Let me lead the team to that building.'

'A life is a life; no life is more precious than another. We are all human when we shed the rank.'

The Captain shouted over the sound of fire, 'Cover us.' He pointed to four men. 'You, you, you and you; on me. Our objective is to get to that building and have two fronts to attack. Let's go!' Captain Sholae and his men shot at the insurgents as they ran for the building. The others laid cover fire.

Though the men respected their Captain, their respect for him just doubled.

As the Captain led his team, a bullet grazed his arm, but he didn't stop. He kept moving; he kept shooting. One of the four men with him saw an insurgent pull the pin off a grenade. 'Grenade!' he screamed and they all dove for cover. He shot twice, catching the insurgent in the head and chest. The grenade did not make it far. It fell amid some insurgents; the resulting explosion killed a good number of them. All five soldiers used the explosion as a smokescreen and made it to the side of the building.

'Sir, we are running out of ammo.'

'Then make every fucking bullet count,' the Captain said and kept shooting.

'What is our exfil plan, sir?'

'I'm thinking.'

The Sergeant had led another group of five to another building, so they now fought from three fronts. The Captain gave the Sergeant a thumbs up and went back to the task at hand. The issue of their depleting ammo was foremost on his mind. Without ammunition, they were toast. There was only one option; they needed to get ammo from the enemy. The Captain tapped a soldier and pointed at the dead insurgents, 'We need to get their ammo.'

'Okay sir. I'll go with someone…'

'Let's go,' the Captain said. Then facing the others, he said, 'Give us cover fire!'

The grenade that exploded earlier had dampened the morale of the insurgents close to the Captain's team. So, it was easy for the Captain and his man to get ammo from the fallen insurgents. They were not too shocked to see some of the dead insurgents in military camouflage. The Captain went thrice to get ammo and weapons from the enemy. The Sergeant had done the same with his team. The central team, from which the other two broke out, provided cover fire. The Captain and Sergeant sent some stash to the central team to augment their ammo.

A truck rolled into the village and the Captain's heart sank. The insurgents had RPGs. The Captain decided it was best the soldiers spread out, so as not to become easy targets. The exchange of fire continued, and they held on as long as they could. The first RPG hit, killing a sergeant and the men with him. The Captain and other soldiers continued fighting gallantly, but they knew they would not survive without backup. It was time to beat a tactical retreat. The Captain shot a path through and started escaping with the four men with him.

As he ran, Captain Sholae heard the insurgents chanting that they had captured an officer. He told his men to go ahead; he would go back and rescue the officer. The four soldiers followed him. 'I told you boys to go!' the Captain shouted in anger as he stopped.

'Sir, we can't let you go alone. We know what we signed up for. We will not abandon you, sir. We follow you even if it is to the death.'

And one of the soldiers quoted from a poem, 'Brother, when you raise your shield, so will I. Sister, when you charge the enemy, so will I. And if death awaits us, calling his warriors home, let me die smiling by your side; for we are family.'

The Captain was speechless as tears welled up in his eyes. He sighed deeply and gave a smart salute. He said, 'I am proud to have fought by your side, sirs. Let's make our nation believe again!'

The five soldiers rushed at the enemy. They could see their comrade kneeling before the insurgents. On sighting the advancing soldiers; one of the insurgents shot the lieutenant in the head. One by one, the four men fell, but they made sure a good number of the vandals left the world with them. The Captain kept going and shooting despite the bullets that had hit him. The insurgents laughed at him as he crawled towards the men with the RPGs. One hand was stretched as if in plea. The Captain was the last soldier alive.

IV

Across the nation, hundreds of kilometres away, Captain Sholae's wife felt a sharp pain in her heart. Her son, who had been playing, suddenly began to cry and ask for his daddy. 'Daddy. My daddy!'

The Captain's wife held her son to her bosom and said into his ear, 'Daddy is fine. He is keeping the country safe for us. He will soon come back home. Your daddy is a warrior, just like you.'

The boy calmed down, but his mother muttered a prayer for her husband in her heart. She hoped he was alright.

One of the insurgents pulled out a machete ready to chop the captain's head off. The Captain knelt in front of the group, and they all gathered around him. He was bloodied; he was panting; he was losing consciousness. The executioner stepped forward, machete raised. The Captain kept mumbling some words; his hands clutched in his mid-section all the while. As the machete came down, the Captain flung his hands with difficulty on either side of him. Two grenades rolled in each direction. 'Grenade!' screamed one of the insurgents.

'Lord, help my country and keep my family,' the Captain said, as the grenades exploded, killing him and the remaining insurgents.

The next day, a car pulled into Captain Sholae's driveway in 177 Battalion Barracks, Keffi. Captain Sholae's wife was elated because she was expecting her mother that morning. She opened the door and saw a staff car; a soldier wearing the rank of Major and a female soldier dressed in ceremonial outfit were walking towards her. She fell to her knees and screamed as she shook her head from side to side, 'No, no, no. Please God, no!' She struggled to her feet and made to run back into the house.

She felt that if the Major did not get to her, whatever bad news he had come with would remain unsaid and not become truth. She ran. The Major caught her before she fell again. There was deep sorrow in his eyes as he willed himself to say the words. Mrs Sholae knew her beloved was gone forever; their son would grow up without his father. Her world had crashed. Captain Sholae had finished his course, for God and country.

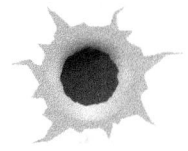

ANYEBE

I

It was a moonless night and the village lay quiet; there was hardly anyone about. The villagers were mostly farmers who tended crops during the day and slept deeply after a good night's meal.

On moonlit nights, children played together in groups or sat around the village story-teller, listening to some folktale with rapt attention. Usually, the adults sat in groups talking about recent events. Some, however, were content to sit alone in front of their houses sipping palm wine. The not-so-young courted in the shadows. Eventually, everyone withdrew into their houses, said their night prayers and retired to bed.

But moonless nights hardly witnessed anyone about. Perhaps, it was the fear of spirits or the absence of the moon's comforting glow that made such nights quiescent. Only hunters and people up to mischief roamed about on such a night.

A pregnant woman lay awake beside her snoring husband; unable to sleep because of his snores. She imagined herself putting a pillow over his head or stuffing a rag into his open mouth, but she loved him too much. So, she nudged him; he grunted two times before the loud snores turned to soft ones. Otali knew that her husband, Olotuche, would soon resume sounding like a cassava grinding machine, so she woke him and told him she wanted to eat bush meat.

'You say?' Olotuche said in unbelief, sleep still in his eyes.

'I want bush meat. That is what is hungrying me,' Otali responded calmly.

'But it is past midnight Otali! Where I will get bush meat at this hour?' The man scratched his crotch with his right hand and covered his mouth with the same hand to stifle a yawn.

'This your child in my stomach,' Otali touched her abdomen, 'that is what he wants to eat.'

'And where do you want me to get bush meat?'

Otali didn't speak. She simply looked at the corner where Olotuche's gun lay and rested her hand on her bulging midriff.

Olotuche got up from the bed and looked at his wife intently. 'We are not having any more children after this.'

'I have heard, my husband; when the time comes, we will see. Just go and bring me bush meat before this baby starts to tangle up my intestines.'

Olotuche dressed up, carried his dane gun and stormed out of the house. He murmured under his breath, 'When the time comes, we will see now. Maybe she will rape me.'

Inside the house, Otali, adjusted herself on the bed and went to sleep. Olotuche would be furious if he ever found out that she sent him into the night because of his snoring. She needed to get as much sleep as she could before he came back.

Outside, Olotuche could hear light snores coming from various houses and he began to miss his bed. He was walking past a house when he heard rhythmic moans. The house belonged to a young unmarried woman who was rumoured to take any man for a small fee. Olotuche looked around and walked quietly to the window where the moaning was coming from. He peeped and saw the two bodies tangled and moving in sync. Olotuche had an erection the whole time, and did not seem to be able to help himself. He knew watching people in the throes of passion was wrong, but Otali was never in the mood these days. It had been a whole five days since they last made love. When the man grunted loudly and fell limp beside the woman, Olotuche forgot himself and said, 'Chai, see as you people are enjoying.'

The lovers in the room looked around wildly and Olotuche ran away from the window.

Olotuche moved into the woods. He heard some sounds from another side of the bush; he saw a flashlight and thought it was a hunter, or another unlucky husband who had got the same odd midnight request. He did not call out for fear of scaring away game. So, Olotuche went his way, deep into the bush.

Not long, Olotuche sighted a rabbit and aimed. The sound of gunfire that burst out was not his own. It was rapid and automatic. Screams chased the sound of the guns – all of it coming from the village. The forest came alive with the sounds of animals scampering for safety. Olotuche started to run back to the village. They were under attack, perhaps from the dreaded armed herdsmen.

A group of men walked into Olotuche's village brandishing Kalash-nikovs and double-edged knives. Two men poured petrol around the village. One kept watch while the others went from house to house spreading death like fire in the harmattan. No one was spared, except those who escaped through the window and made it past the vandals who stood watch. Women, children and men lay dead in their homes or the open.

Otali was awake and scared. Why had she sent her husband to the bush this very night? She heard a noise and waddled to the door, her hand over her protruded stomach. When she opened, the first thing that came into her house was the muzzle of a gun, then the whole barrel; then a man, not Olotuche behind the gun. The man behind the gun had a wicked grin. The man behind the gun had an erection. The man behind the gun raped her to his heart's content. The man behind the gun sliced her stomach open afterwards. The man behind the gun was leaving the house when the front door of the house opened violently and hit him in the face.

Olotuche charged into his house and collided with a man who had a gun and a long knife. The gun and knife had fallen across the room. Olotuche wrestled the man to the ground and knocked him unconscious. Olotuche took one look at his wife gasping for breath, her stomach split open and decided to wait. He waited quietly till the man stirred then he picked up the long knife and plunged it into the murderer's chest repeatedly. After that, he staggered back against the wall and slid to the ground; he watched his wife through teary eyes.

The other assailants noticed one of them was missing and be-gan a search; for some reason they were not in a hurry. As they ap-proached Olotuche's house, the door flew open. Olotuche walked out with his dane gun strapped to his back and the automatic weapon aimed and ready. He shot at the insurgents and killed two; the others ran behind a building. Olotuche was too angry to seek cover. He did not know that the men who ran away would cut him off from behind. Soon, his body was riddled with bullets and he fell to the floor. As life ebbed out of him, he turned his head towards his house; his eyes seeking his wife's.

In the morning, when the news spread, people would see a man in open space, his body riddled with holes and the ground beneath him darkened by his own blood. They would see that he was looking towards a house and they would go there and find the gory sight of a woman whose stomach had been slit open and foetus hanging out of it.

II

'Killer herdsmen invade a community in Gwer East Local Government…' It was the same story of gloom as the news anchor stated the casualty figure. The news showed the footage of a village burnt to the ground, with people leaving their homes in fear and going to seek refuge in the state capital. Families had suffered irreparable damage; the survivors would never be the same. The killers had no code, no honour, and no discernible cause. They were simply a band of despoilers on rampage. The security operatives seemed to be at a loss. There were even claims that they were colluding with the insurgents. A retired General had advised everyone to take up arms and protect themselves. His words had been severely criticised by the government.

A retired Special Forces operative, Colonel Abel Ogidi (Rtd.) was horrified at the news. The attack had come close to his village. He knew if something was not done soon, his village and everyone in it would perish. He decided to do something about it. He picked his phone and called some of the men with whom he had served with in the army. He would prepare his people.

Col. Abel drove into his community with Captain Usman, Lieutenant Pamilerin and Sergeant Steven. They had served under the Colonel's leadership in the Potiskum sector before they all decided they'd had enough. They deeply respected the Colonel and had always responded to his call to socialise. Now he had called them to fight. Their first port of call was the palace of the Village Head. The old man was glad to see the son of the soil who had come with friends to help his people protect themselves. The old man prayed for the four warriors, and for peace and respite from impending danger. The town crier was told to invite all able-bodied men to the village square by noon the next day.

The soldiers stayed with the Colonel's grandmother. The woman had refused to leave the village. She had seen many sorrows. First, Abel's mother had gotten pregnant with him at sixteen, and died at childbirth. Then her husband had died under strange circumstances. But she had persevered, and the village had been her solace. She was determined to die in the village and be buried next to her husband. She prepared a sumptuous meal for the men and listened to her grandson's plan. When they had eaten, she prayed for them and told them that she was not afraid to die. She was simply afraid that her husband's grave would be desecrated and her homeland overrun by vandals.

Word spread about the reason for the meeting in the village square. So, by noon the next day, the village square was full. Men, women, and even aged people showed up. Those who were not expected to be there did not want to leave; everyone wanted to know what they had to do to be safe and how they could help. Colonel Abel decided to give a little talk about safety and how everyone could play a part. He told the villagers not to go into the bush alone and to raise an alarm when they saw a strange face. Further instructions would be given later.

After the talk, the Colonel, as he was now called, asked all able bodied men above fifteen years to stay behind. He told the men that it was up to them to defend their village and people. They would be given a crash course in military strategy and tactics. They would learn how to handle guns and use any weapon at their disposal as a means of protection.

The training was intense. In a few days, they dug trenches and laid traps at every entrance to the village. Colonel Abel and his men prepared handmade explosives and kept them at strategic points just outside the community. They also procured some weapons which they gave to men who showed promise during marksmanship training. Everyone knew his role and was determined to play his part. It was time to get to work.

They came at midnight, through the bushes, armed with rifles and machetes and kegs of petrol. The intruders went from house to house raping, breaking, killing and burning. The night was pierced with gunfire and screams. The few who managed to escape from their houses were hacked down with machetes.

In Abel's village, two men on guard duty heard the shots and screams and quickly surmised that the village beside theirs was under attack. The Colonel called some of his best men and proceeded to the next village. Other men were to stay back and secure their village. Abel and the selected men made for the village under attack, the better to attack the problem from afar before it came to take a seat in their domain. As they moved, Abel told them the plan.

The men moved in pairs and were positioned at the two entrances to the attacked village. Two men took to the trees to act as snipers. As the men entered into the village, Abel heard a man slumped to the ground behind him. He had been taken out by a sniper in the trees. Another man was taken out right in the village square.

Abel and one of his men chased after two terrorists. Unfortunately, they had a little boy as hostage. One of the terrorist had his gun on the child's head while the other told Abel, 'One more step and the child dies! Drop your guns!'

Abel and Steven had their guns trained on each of the terrorists. 'Let the boy go and we might let you live,' Abel replied calmly.

'You think we are joking,' the terrorist with the gun said, 'I will kill the child. I swear by Allah, I will kill the child.'

'Don't mention Allah. He does not support the evil you do.' Steven said matter-of-factly.

The terrorist pressed his gun against the lad's head; Col Abel saw him fingering the trigger.

Abel was quiet for a while and began to hum a tune as he stepped back. Steven thought his boss had gone mad; the terrorists thought so too. A shot rang out.

One of the snipers in the trees had shot the terrorist holding the boy in the back. His colleague panicked and was quickly shot in the chest by Steven. The boy dove for cover and Abel shot twice. Steven realised the tune Abel hummed was a war song in his local dialect; one of their snipers had picked the song and knew what to do. When Abel and his men got to the village to see the situation of things, they saw the boy crying beside the corpse of his mother.

Abel and his men went back to his village and notified everyone to prepare for an attack soon. Abel knew the terrorists would seek revenge. He knew the terrorists would get word that men in his village were armed and had even constituted themselves into a vigilante force, neutralising threats around them. His village had to be ready. Abel also knew his village would have a problem with the security operatives. They had gathered the arms and ammunition from the dead terrorists, and Abel knew the security operatives would soon start asking questions. The army had been directed to mop up arms in the wrong hands. Abel and his men hid their weapons in a safe place. He decided that when the army comes, he would lead them off the scent. If it came to it, he would pull a few strings. He knew people high up and his exploits in the North-East had not been forgotten.

The killer herdsmen came for their revenge an hour after midnight, three days later. They came in minivans, with guns and kegs of petrol. Their first port of call was the village Col. Abel and his men had helped liberate. The people of the village put up some resistance, but their machetes and crude farm tools were no match for their assailants' AK47s. Women and children were forced to watch their men die before the terrorists turned on them.

A brother and sister made it out and ran into the forest; they made for Abel's village. The brother noticed that two of the terrorists were on their tail. He hid his sister and doubled back on their assailants. With his machete, he hacked down one of the terrorists who was getting close to where his sister was hiding. He had just turned when the other terrorist showed up and shot him in the arm. The boy was in pain, but ran back towards their village, giving his sister a chance to live and to get help from Abel's village. The boy had told his sister to run to the other village no matter what. 'Live for the both of us,' he shouted. The boy ran into his village and killed two more of the terrorists before being gunned down.

The girl got to Abel's village just before dawn and collapsed. When she came to, she shared the story of horror. The villagers looked to Abel. Abel assured the people and reminded them of all the security measures they had been taught. After that, Abel went with two of his best men to the village just attacked. All that was left were charred ruins, and a few survivors foraging for anything they could salvage. They shook their heads and wondered if they were the ones who brought complete annihilation to the village.

When Abel and his men got back to his village, he went to the Village Head. 'Anyone who wants to leave should do so now because these killer herdsmen are coming; they will be here tonight in all their might. Women, children and the aged should go somewhere safe. The same goes for any man who does not want blood on his hands.'

Buses had been arranged and they filled up quickly. Abel's grandmother refused to leave. 'I will be your spiritual guide,' she said, 'I might not be able to fight physically, but I will do so in prayer!'

'Mama, you can do so where you are going. Go to my house in the city.' A frustrated Abel said.

'No, I will not leave my kin and my land. Also if any of you get injured, who will patch you up!' and then she added, with a hint of pride in her eyes, 'In case you have forgotten, I retired as a Chief Matron.'

Abel and the men watched the buses leave. There was no judgement for the men who left in the buses. He understood. After the buses left, he called those who stayed behind and told them the battle plan.

Abel, Pamilerin, Steven and Usman sat at the centre of the village. They told the civilians among them to get enough sleep because it was going to be a long night. This was after they set more trap and mines. Abel looked at his brothers in arms and said, 'None of you have to stay back, you know. There is still time to leave.'

'And leave you all by yourself; I don't think so, sir,' Sergeant Steven (Rtd.) said.

'We are with you, no matter what,' Lieutenant Pamilerin (Rtd.) said, nodding to the other men.

'We will follow you anywhere, sir. Through the gates of hell if need be,' Captain Usman (Rtd.) said, and then added, 'These men are monsters and giving my people a bad name!'

Col. Abel rose to his feet and all he could say was, 'Alright then. Let's give these bastards the fight of their lives. Ahua!'

'Ahua!' the men responded.

The Colonel and his men patrolled the village. A few men were asked to stand sentry at every entrance to the village. Each man was given a whistle which he was to blow if he sighted any strange activity. The Colonel had told them not to try to engage the hostiles alone. As the Colonel was moving to the village square, he heard a sound from behind a building. He dashed behind the building and saw a figure run. The Colonel gave chase and caught a little boy who tried to wriggle out of his hands. 'Hey, calm down,' Col. Abel tried to pacify the boy.

'Leave me, leave me!' the boy screamed.

'Okay, okay, but calm down. If you are calm, I will let you go.'

The boy relaxed and the Colonel eased his grip. The boy was breathing heavily, but still sat there; the Colonel behind him. The Colonel placed an arm on the boy's shoulder and said, 'You should have gone with the others!'

The boy burst into tears and told his story.

The boy's name was Anyebe and he was not from Abel's village. His village had been attacked and his parents had died. His mother followed him through a path behind their house while his father went to fight the invaders.

'Run, my son. I am behind you!'

He ran into the forest and kept looking back to make sure his mother was close. He was beginning to worry after a while and was tempted to turn back when he saw her outline. 'Run!' she charged.

He ran and when he was tired, she picked him up and they ran further into the forest.

She was gasping and it was then he looked at his hands which had been wrapped around her, they were sticky from her blood.

'Mummy!' he shrilled, as he stared into her eyes.

His mother gave him a weak smile. 'My son, my brave and beautiful son.'

Anyebe began to cry.

'Look at me, son,' his mother beckoned, 'You are alive and that is what is important. Live my son; make sure you survive and live. Go to that village and tell them your story, they will help you.'

'Mummy, please don't die'

With her breathing laboured, she whispered, 'I will always be with you, Anyebe. Live free.' She took a deep breath and she stopped moving.

When the boy was done, Col. Abel asked him, 'Why didn't you join the buses when you saw them going to the city?'

'I don't know anyone in the city, sir. Also I want to help,' and looking pleadingly into Abel's face and in a low tone, he added, 'Please sir, let me help in any way I can.'

Abel looked at this boy who had lost both parents and had been robbed of his childhood. Abel led the boy to his grandmother's house and told him to protect her.

'Thank you, sir. I will keep her safe,' Anyebe said, determined.

Abel gave him a smart salute and the boy did same. He left the house and went to go over final strategies with the men.

The terrorists came early in the evening, in five trucks. They all had their faces covered with scarfs. They had machetes, knives, guns and some explosives. And as always, they had gallons of petrol for arson. They were really cocky and did nothing to hide their advance. Col. Abel who held fort at the entrance of the village with the Alpha Team spoke quietly into his radio, 'We have tangos inbound in five vans; they are heavily armed. So get ready to repel on my mark.'

They waited for the last van to drive past a mine they had set. The mines went off, boxing the intruders in. The gasoline in the vans aided the explosion. A good number of the insurgents were blown to bits.

'Advance!' Colonel Abel yelled, and the men with him went into action.

They moved through the flames and killed the insurgents; using the smoke as cover. One of the villagers got hit in the arm and fell down in pain; Abel shot the shooter and was just helping his comrade up when he heard a grunt behind him. He turned back just in time to see one of the terrorists fall to the ground. A sniper had shot him in the head. Abel saw his assailant's hand open and a pear shaped object rolled out. 'Grenade!' he screamed, jumping out of the way; and it exploded. When the dust settled, the Colonel had lost a man to the explosion. Colonel Abel and his men picked the weapons they could salvage including two Rocket Propelled Grenade launchers and continued to engage the vandals. With the weaponry the vandals had, the Colonel and his men no longer looked at the men as cow herders, they were armed bandits as far as the Colonel and his men were concerned.

Silence soon descended but Colonel Abel knew it would be short lived. He knew that the insurgents had gone to regroup; he had told his men not to let down their guard. Abel was still trying to assess damage to his men, when Steven shouted, 'Contact front.' Soon they were engaging the enemies on more than one front.

Their snipers were picking off tangos one after another, but it would not last very long. One of the men sighted an insurgent with a rocket launcher and shouted, 'RPG!' The men on the ground took cover, but the target was one of the snipers on the tree. When the rocket hit, the impact flung the man into the bush. He did not survive.

Abel's men fired some RPGs of their own, but the size of the enemy did not seem to shrink. Some of the intruders had made it into the village from an unmanned entrance into the village. The entry was unmanned because it led to a very steep slope, and hardly did anyone come through there. But the intruders risked life and limb to make the climb. They sneaked into the town and made their way into the square flanking Abel and his team from the side. Soon, Abel and his team were combatting enemies from three sides.

The men huddled up and were trying to come up with another strategy. They were oblivious of the automatic weapon trained on them. An intruder hid behind one of the buildings and wore a cynical grin. He had them where he wanted them. A finger caressed the trigger and then…

One of the intruders made for a house that had a light on. He kicked open the door to see an old woman sitting with her bible opened in front of her. He had a wicked grin as he raised his rifle. The intruder walked slowly towards the old woman and placed the muzzle of the gun on her temple.

The old woman spoke to the terrorist about Christ. The terrorist paused in admiration of her faith. 'You are not afraid to die?'

'No, for I am not like them who have no hope. If I die, I know where I am going,' then Abel's grandmother asked, 'If you die, do you know where you are going?'

The terrorist lowered the gun.

Abel and his men heard a shrill as an intruder walked uncoordinatedly into the open and fell down to the ground dead. Some of the men shot him just to make sure. Anyebe walked out into the open, a pistol in his hand. One question formed on Abel's lips, 'Where is my grandmother?'

Anyebe ran towards the old woman's house even as Abel and two other men followed him.

Abel barged in, gun on the ready. He stopped short in his track as he stared at the sight before him. His grandmother and the terrorist had a bible between them as they studied. The terrorist had tears in his eyes as he listened with rapt attention. Abel took a deep breath and let it out slowly.

Captain Usman led the Charlie team into the woods; blending in the darkness as they took out the enemy. Usman leaned against a tree and one of the intruders backed into him. The intruder heard a soft grunt; he turned on the Captain in one swift movement, his finger squeezing the trigger even as he screamed in both fright and anger. Usman side stepped causing the terrorist to shoot past him. He plunged the knife in the man's chest. He whistled and his team made back for the village.

Lieutenant Pamilerin and the Delta team shot at the enemy from trenches they had dug. One of his men ran out of the trench and killed a good number of vandals. He was shot multiple times, but he kept going as the bullets did not have an effect on him. Another member of Pamilerin's team wanted to do same. He died before he got within a hundred meters. This one did not have the local charm to work for him.

The charmed man wreaked havoc against the terrorists with his machete when his gun chamber hit empty. Then he stopped as an RPG stared at him. His charm was meant for bullets, but he let go of caution as he continued his onward charge. The man was obliterated. The RPG was now aimed at the trench that served as cover for Pamilerin and his team. Some of the men had run out of the trench, away from cover and had been gunned down.

Abel joined the other men in the fight. He shot at the advancing enemy and asked, 'Where is Pamilerin?'

Pamilerin watched as the RPG was aimed at the trench. He aimed and shot high at a massive branch. It landed on the shooter. The RPG did not get far and killed a good number of the terrorists. In the confusion, Lieutenant Pamilerin and his team ran back to the village to join the others.

III

Dead bodies littered everywhere in the village. Both sides had lost men, but the greater loss was with the vandals'. Though a good number of the vandals were dead, Abel knew those of them who survived would go for reinforcement. And he knew that the backup would be bigger and more vengeful than the initial force. It was time to take a decision.

Abel spoke to his men. 'Men, you have all fought gallantly today. But I don't think we can hold off for much longer. Me, Usman, Pamilerin and Steven have real combat experience and will stay behind. The rest of you, please go and get help. There is a path at the back of the village; you can sneak away through there.'

No one moved.

Abel faced Anyebe, 'You need to get out of here now, boy!'

'I will stay with you and fight!' Anyebe responded. The other men echoed his response.

'You don't understand. We appreciate your valour, but we need help. We won't survive without help. There is a military outpost not far from here. We need you people to go there and tell them we need help.'

Still, no one moved.

Abel looked at the men and selected four men to stay. He told the remaining men that they were on a mission; their mission was to survive and get help. He asked the men to get to the nearest military outpost or police station and call for help. As the men left, the Colonel called Anyebe back.

'Anyebe you wanted to help. This is your chance. Make sure you survive and send help.'

Anyebe and the men left through the forest; they could hear a vehicle coming. From the engine sound, they could tell it was a truck. They ran; they prayed for their comrade with every step, and pleaded with providence that they would find the help they needed.

The truck was parked sideways at the entrance of the village. All the men on the truck got off leaving just two men who mounted a .50 calibre automatic weapon. Abel and his men could see it from where they took cover. 'We cannot survive that, if they unleash,' Usman said forthrightly.

Abel took a deep breath and said, 'If we don't survive this, we'll die knowing we did the best we could. We will die as warriors.'

The men around him nodded solemnly.

The terrorists heard someone calling to them and saw the terrorist who had been with Abel's grandmother. He walked to the group, a bloodied knife in his hand. He bragged that he had just killed a woman related to the leader of the resistance. Abel sat heavily on the ground and took laboured breaths. His men tried to console him, but his mind was far away.

The insurgents were cheering their comrade and patting him as he joined them by the truck. Abel and his men ran out of hiding with the intention of firing at the enemy. There was a loud explosion as the truck blew up. Abel and his men could hear death screams even as some terrorists were on fire. Abel did not understand. He rushed to his grandmother's house and saw her praying. She was praying for the convert who gave his life so they could have a little more time. Abel told his grandmother to hide in her bedroom. He made barricades and left through the window. 'You are not to come out of this room, no matter what happens. Help I know, will come.'

Anyebe ran without stopping. The boy refused to let the fatigue get to him. They had all split up, with some going to neighbouring villages to ask for help too. Anyebe ran for the military post Abel had spoken about. When he got there, the sentry ordered him to stop or get shot. Anyebe raised his hands high above his head, waving a white singlet as he shouted, 'We need help. They are going to kill them!'

The sentry moved cautiously towards him and asked him to slowly lift his shirt up and turn around. When the sentry was satisfied he had no bomb vest, he told Anyebe to tell him what was amiss. The sentry went to the leader of his team. 'Colonel Abel is in trouble, sir.'

A good name they say is better than gold. Abel had been a great soldier when he served and his reputation preceded him wherever he went. Some soldiers got into two vans led by their leader. He instructed some men to wait behind and radio their base. As they rode, all the soldiers prayed that they would not be too late.

Abel and his men were lucky because the blown up truck did a lot of damage to the enemies' number. The men advanced, taking cover and returning fire. It was only a matter of time before... 'I'm down to my last clip,' was the shout from most of the men.

'Hold your fire!' ordered Abel, 'We retreat back into the village. Let them come to us and we pick them out. Three short bursts and make every bullet count!'

Abel said, 'I want four men on the side of that building. They need to come between these two buildings if they want to get at us. This is where we make our stand!'

The men could hear the terrorists approaching. Abel raised a fist as a signal for his men to hold fire. He counted to three before pointing forward. They unleashed on the enemy when they were in range. The terrorists had no cover.

'We won't be able to hold them off much longer, sir. Do we have an exfil plan?' Steven yelled, over the sound of fire power.

'No, we don't. I hope help is on its way,' Abel said.

They continued to hold off the enemy, but lost two of the men with them.

Abel fired the last two RPGs and then heard the words he feared, 'I'm out!' The men pulled out their knives; they were determined to fight to their deaths. Abel and the other five braced themselves for hand combat even as the adrenaline coursed through their veins. Suddenly, they heard loud shouts and the enemy retreating. The men stepped out and through the smoke; they saw farmers and hunters from neighbouring villages brandishing cutlasses, rakes, spades, sickles, dane guns and the likes. Close behind them was a group of soldiers led by Anyebe. Abel stood there; tears of joy falling down his face.

The terrorists were decimated and a few caught, Abel went to his grandmother and helped her out of the house. She made him sit down while she dressed his wound; as she did, she kept saying prayers of thanksgiving. Anyebe rushed into the old woman's arms, crying for joy. The men helped bury the dead. The soldiers spoke to their comrades; laughing and joyous that the end was good.

IV

The sounds of sirens pierced the atmosphere of the village. The police had come, late as usual.

'Which one of you is Abel?' the police chief asked when they parked.

Pamilerin, Usman and Steven stepped forward. 'Who wants to know?' Pamilerin asked.

'I am Colonel Abel,' the Colonel answered.

The police chief looked at the four men and said, 'Arrest him.'

'Sir?' one of the policemen said.

'I said arrest him, arrest them all. No one should take the law into their own hands. He should have called security agents and waited. We cannot have mayhem in our communities. We even heard he distributed guns!'

A group of soldiers stood in front of the four men and told the policemen, 'If they born una papa well, make una touch am. Just try nonsense!'

The policemen went back to their leader, 'Sir, iz like they will not allow us arrest them o!'

'This is a military issue,' one of the soldiers said. 'Go back to law enforcement and leave us with peace keeping.'

But the police chief was adamant and said it was within his jurisdiction to retrieve illegal arms from the civilian population. He further said that Abel had finished his service in the army and could not be arming civilians.

A fracas had nearly broken out between the police and the soldiers when Abel stopped it.

'I'll go with these men,' he said. 'Let me go and explain myself to the police.'

Facing the policemen, Abel said, 'I take full responsibility for everything that happened here today. These men acted on my orders as they were trained to, so please leave them out of this.'

Usman, Pamilerin and Steven wanted to protest, but Abel gave them a look and nodded at them to keep quiet.

As Abel was led away, he asked Usman to take his grandmother and Anyebe to his house in the city. The soldiers formed a guard of honour and saluted him. There was a shout. 'Wait, wait.' Everyone froze as Anyebe led the old woman to her grandson. 'I am proud of you Abel. Everyone here knows what you did and we will testify if need be. God be with you and bless you, my son.' She hugged him and then moved out of the way. Anyebe stood in front of Abel and stared for a while; he placed his feet together and with his back straight, gave a smart salute. Abel smiled as he saluted the best he could with the cuffs.

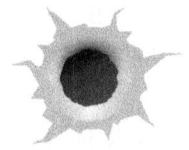

TWO DAYS

I

He adjusted the lens on his Laptop. 'Can you see me now?'

'Yes honey, we see you,' Abel's wife replied, her gap-toothed smile taking up the screen. The two-year old boy on her lap had a toy in his mouth. He was not interested in the face on the screen.

'How are you, my love?' Abel asked.

'Better, now that I see you.'

'Our boy is massive. What are you feeding him?'

Lieutenant Colonel Abel made his wife smile with his questions. She laughed out loud when he asked if their son had a girlfriend yet. He was in the North East and far from home. He had been away for eighteen months; fighting insurgents and striving for peace.

'Honey, you look lean, and there are bags under your eyes. Are you eating? Are you sleeping at all?' Abel's wife said. 'And you need to shave.'

Abel laughed and replied, 'Babe, we are not at the Hilton over here. We are in enemy territory most of the time, trying to stay alive and make this country safe for everyone.'

'I know. But you need to take good care of yourself, please.'

'I will,' he replied, a huge smile on his lips.

Lt. Col Abel missed his family. He was grateful that his tour would be over in two days. He wanted to surprise his wife, so he did not tell her. He spoke with his wife for a few more minutes while their son made baby sounds in the background. Just before the link disconnected, the baby touched the screen and said, 'Ba-ba.' It was all the proud parents could do not to break into tears. Abel was happy; he felt like he could float as he walked out of the communications tent.

A sergeant ran to him, saluted and told him the commanding officer wanted to see him immediately. He walked to the CO's office. The man was like a father to everyone under his command.

In the CO's office, Lt. Col. Abel saluted smartly and was asked to sit. The CO fixed himself a drink and poured Abel a glass. The two men sipped their drinks quietly. While sipping the drinks, the CO said nothing. He simply stared into space, turning this way and that on his swivel chair.

'Sir, is anything the matter?' Abel was worried.

Brigadier General Oluseyi turned his chair to face Abel, 'I'm fine. There is nothing wrong. You must be looking forward to the end of your tour.'

'Yes, sir. My men and I are looking forward to seeing our families soon.' Abel added, 'You should be going home yourself in two weeks, sir.'

'Yes, I should.' The commander smiled.

'Sir, why am I here?' Abel asked when the General kept making small talk.

'Always one for a direct assault,' the General said, and sighed deeply, 'I need you for one last job before you and your men leave.'

Abel sat up, 'What type of job, sir?'

'I know you are due to go home in two days, but I need you to extend an extra day. We are expecting a guest, and she will require escorts.'

'Sir, I believe there are teams who can handle it,' Abel said. His tone was a mix of assertion and care. He did not want to upset his commander.

The General got up and walked to Abel's side before sitting on the edge of the table. 'The Senate President's daughter wants to visit an IDP camp in this sector. She picked a camp close to us, and I have been instructed to keep her safe.'

'Any of the teams on the ground could do it, sir.'

'I know. But I want my best men on the job. Your team is the best I have,' the General said.

'Sir...' Abel started but was cut short.

'I understand your concern, especially because you are going home in two days. But we don't expect any trouble. We all know what happened to Abu Ali and the others; we don't want to lose any more men if we can help it.'

Abel took a deep breath as he remembered his friend, Sarkin Yaki, the warrior. All the soldiers missed his leadership.

'Sir, when does she arrive?'

'She should be here tomorrow by 1245hrs. We will have a meeting with her so we can map out her path and come up with strategies to prevent any funny business.'

'Yes, sir. I'll brief my team.'

'Abel, I know they will be disappointed. Let them know it was last minute, and I wouldn't have made the call if it wasn't absolutely necessary.'

'I understand sir.' Abel saluted and left.

Back in their room, Major Okon faced his leader and said, 'Extension by an extra day, Oga.'

Abel looked up and said, 'Who said anything about an extension? Okon, you have been snooping around and poking your nose where it does not belong, again.'

'Oga, that is why you asked me to join your team, sir. Information gathering, to get intel before anyone does.'

Abel sighed heavily.

'Sir, so it is true.' Lieutenant Usman said.

'It is,' Abel said soberly.

'Osalobua, which kain wahala be dis?' Osaz exploded.

Lieutenant Emeka hissed loudly and began to sulk.

'Guys, give Oga chance to explain na.' Captain Rotimi said.

'The Senate President's daughter is coming to visit an IDP camp near us. We are to serve as her escorts.'

'Sir, I'm sure another team can handle it.' A visibly frustrated Osaz stated.

'Oga told the CO, but the General said he wants his best men on the job,' Okon butt in.

Abel glared at him, 'Okon, must you be so good at what you do? What is wrong with you?'

'Oga, is the girl hot?' Captain Rotimi asked, his eyes lighting up.

Everyone turned to face him in bewilderment.

'Wetin? I dey ask if the babe set, una dey look me. No be wetin all of una dey reason be dat? Abegi.'

'No go marry, you hear? Dey do fine boy up and down.' Major Okon said, causing everyone to laugh.

'Why be say na only me una go dey call? Emeka sef never marry,' Rotimi tried to vindicate himself.

'Ehn? You don forget say I give you wedding invitation, abi. I dey commot from una association of bachelors next two weeks. Go find another person wey you go use join body,' Emeka replied.

They all laughed, except Rotimi.

Lt. Col. Abel cleared his voice. He had listened to his men's banter enough. He loved the men in the team. Though they had different ranks, the men behaved like brothers.

'Guys,' Abel said, 'let's do this last mission and go home. Our loved ones are waiting for us.' The men nodded.

'Carry on,' Abel said.

The men saluted, and Abel stepped out into the night to pray.

II

The military chopper bearing the Senate President's daughter touched down at one o'clock in the afternoon. Once she alighted, she and her team were escorted to meet the CO and some high-ranking officers at the base. After a few minutes of pleasantries, The General and Abel sat down to a meeting with her and her aides.

'Funke,' the General said, 'This is Lt. Colonel Abel. He will be leading the team that will escort you to the IDP camp tomorrow.'

'Thank you, uncle. But do you think that will be necessary? I came with my security; they are up to the task,' Funke said.

Abel scoffed and shook his head.

'Excuse me,' Funke addressed Abel. 'Do you have a problem with me!' Funke said with raised eyebrows.

'No, not with you ma'am,' Abel responded, 'your naiveté. This sector is a military hot zone.'

'Excuse me. Did you just call me naïve?'

'I apologise, but what combat experience do your men have? How well do they know this territory?'

'Funke,' the General weighed in, 'he is right. Your men don't know the terrain as we do. Besides, I promised your father and my sister to keep you safe, and Abel is the best I have.'

'I don't like him; he does not look like much; I bet my men can take him,' Funke eyed Abel.

'I'd like to see them try,' Abel said with a wicked grin.

The CO gave Abel a stern look and turned to his niece. 'Let's get back to keeping you safe.'

'Uncle, this one is rude; I don't want him on my team.'

The Brigadier General sighed in frustration; only to hear Abel say, 'Sorry sweetheart, you are stuck with my team and I. We are your new best friends.'

They stood over a map, and Abel talked to his superior about their best approach. He was particular about keeping the visit under wraps to prevent insurgents from taking advantage. He suggested they go in two Humvees along with the cars the VIP and her team would go in.

The two soldiers seemed to be in a world of their own while Funke and her security details looked on. All the talk about sector and guns and recce felt incomprehensible. They wondered what it was about a simple visit that warranted all the big-sounding clipped words. The General made some observations and turned to his niece.

'So, you will leave tomorrow morning at eight o'clock, in convoy: two Humvees and three Jeeps.'

'Uncle, don't you think eight is a bit early,' Funke said.

Abel tried not to snigger. 'We need to go early so you can leave the place on time. It's just a meet and greet.'

'Okay!' she replied, glaring at Abel.

'And no posting anything until after,' the General added.

'Posting?' Funke sounded confused.

'You know, Facebook, Twitter and whatever social media things you kids are on these days. Please keep your visit here a secret till you leave; when you get home, you can tweet to your heart's content,' Abel explained.

Funke was livid; she rose to her feet and facing her uncle. 'Uncle, if that is all, I'd like to retire so I can get up early tomorrow.'

When the soldiers were left alone, the CO said, 'She is a good girl, Abel. Please keep her safe.'

'Yes, sir.' Abel saluted smartly and left his boss' office.

As soon as the door closed, the General burst out laughing. He remembered Abel's words, '…whatever social media things you kids are on these days.' The General laughed so hard he almost fell off his chair. His Orderly rushed in to find his boss laughing hard. The Orderly was worried that his boss had lost it. PTSD was real! He was about to go for the medic when the General told him not to worry, he was fine. The Orderly looked doubtful, but his principal told him to leave; he was fine.

Immediately Abel got to his men in their room, they started laughing.

'Whatever social media things you kids are on these days? Good one boss,' Emeka said, causing the men more mirth.

Abel glared at Okon.

41

Okon had a straight look. 'It wasn't me, sir.'

'Sir, you told the girl that?' Usman said, trying to control his laughter.

'The girl is spoilt, I tell you.'

'You should have seen her face,' Okon said.

'I thought you said it wasn't you,' Abel said.

Everyone laughed.

'Oga, you did not tell us the girl is fine like that.' Rotimi said.

They all stared at him. Emeka said, 'Go and marry, ashawo!'

'Chai, why una dey do me like this na? Haba, I am just making an observation.'

'Alright, guys. Listen up,' Abel called his men to order and briefed them on the plan.

An hour later, Danladi walked into their room, all smiles. Danladi owed his life to Abel and his team; especially Abel. Some terrorists had attacked his village and sacked it. Abel and his men found Danladi, wounded and left to die. They rescued the boy and brought him to the base's clinic. Abel refused to give up on the boy. He came to after two surgeries and lots of rest. The boy felt he was forever in their debt, despite numerous explanations that they were only doing their job.

'A pine lady iz coming to ze Ai Zee Fee camf tomorrow,' Danladi said to the men.

Abel froze.

'How do you know?' Okon asked.

'It is here on pacebuk,' the boy said, and proudly showed them his phone. The information was on Facebook and Twitter. All the men looked at each other and their leader.

'Oga, please take it easy,' Rotimi said, as Abel was visibly shaking.

Abel walked into his CO's office and told him what had happened.

'Oh my God!' the General said, his head in his hands. 'This child!'

'What do we do now, sir. The whole world knows we will be there tomorrow.'

The General stared into nothingness. He was angry and frustrated at the same time. He picked his phone and put it on speaker.

'Hello, Uncle,' Funke greeted.

'Funke, but Lt. Col. Abel was very clear about you not posting anything on social media until you get home.' the General started.

'Yes sir, but my PA had posted before I got back to the room. She did not know. She is here; she is sorry.'

The General took a deep breath; he was short of words.

'Uncle, are you there?'

'He is here, but does not know what to say to you,' Abel said.

'Oh, you again,' Funke said on the other end.

'Hope your phone is on speaker so your PA can hear us.'

'Not that it is any of your business, but it is.'

'Well, tell her she just killed you all, do you hear? She just put all your lives at risk.'

'How dare you? Do you know who I am? Do you know who my father is?'

'I don't care!'

'I'll report your insolence to my father!'

'Good, maybe he will pick up a gun and come here to fight too!'

'You are…'

'Enough! Both of you,' the General bellowed. 'Your bickering is making it hard for me to think!'

'But Uncle…'

'I said, keep quiet!'

The General sighed and said, 'You will go tomorrow as planned; only now, you will go much earlier. You think eight o'clock is early! See you at five-thirty!'

'But...'

'And don't even think of coming to the rally point late!'

'Yes, sir.'

'And Funke, you will start talking to my men with respect. You just put their lives and yours at risk. Am I clear?'

'Yes, sir.'

The general slammed the phone.

'Sir...' Abel started.

The General raised his hand and said, 'I know, Abel. Please keep her safe. If you go early enough, you should be out of there between 0700hrs to 0730hrs. Please, bring her back in one piece.'

'I'll do my best sir.' Abel saluted and took his leave.

III

At five o'clock in the morning, Abel and his men were geared up and ready to go. The team was at the rally point, going over the plan again for the last time. Abel, Usman and Osaz were to take the lead Humvee; Osaz would handle the gun while Usman drove. The second Humvee would take Okon, Rotimi and Emeka; Emeka would man the gun while Rotimi drove. They heard movement behind them and saw the VIP and her entourage coming towards them. They drove out of the base.

Time check: 0525hrs.

It was an uneventful one-hour trip. They rode into the abandoned school that served as the IDP camp, and the VIP mingled with the IDPs. She was distraught at the state of affairs of the camp as she listened to heart-breaking stories from some of the refugees. She was cross with the coordinators of the camp because she had heard that they diverted food meant for the IDPs for personal use and even sold to them. She spoke to girls who confessed that they had to give their bodies from time to time, to get food and other basics. When they weren't willing to have sex, they were raped, anyway; afterward, they were given the necessities. Funke gave a short address, promising to give feedback to her father on happenings in the camp. She promised them better conditions in no time; also stating that they would all soon return to their homes because the government was working very hard to decimate Boko Haram and restore calm in the area.

Funke served food, as the camera rolled and her aides took pictures. The displaced persons were eating jollof rice that morning. The rice looked rich: at least the one in the warmer Funke was serving from. The campers suspected that the food in the other warmers would not be as rich or well garnished. So, they struggled to get their meal from the visitor. One of Funke's aides stepped in front of the table, trying to keep the crowd orderly. Suddenly, he jerked forward; his head lolled and he fell, dead! Blood oozed out from his body. Funke screamed; the crowd scattered.

Time check: 0715hrs.

Abel and his men were observing at vantage points when they heard the ruckus. People were scampering for safety as those closest to the VIP got shot. Her security operatives surrounded her as she crouched in between them and they made for the cars. The IDPs around them were being taken out one at a time.

Captain Rotimi ran towards the VIP and her aides. He pulled Funke from their midst and moved the other way. The security details had gotten to the car and were about to get in when…Boom!

45

Rotimi and Funke were flung across the school yard, shrapnel falling around them. Abel and the other soldiers had started running towards Rotimi and Funke, but they were having difficulty getting through the mass of bodies running in every direction. Captain Rotimi sat up and shook his head to stop the ringing in his ears. He tried to focus; finally, he remembered where he was. He looked around and saw Funke sprawled some metres from him. He went to her and shook her gently.

Abel and the other men successfully got to the duo and helped them up. Funke was still confused as to what was happening. Abel instructed them to make their way to one of the class blocks. They could still hear people dropping dead around them from the sniper's shots.

'Anybody have eyes on that sniper? I need the bastard taken out!'

'On it,' Osaz replied.

'I'll go with him,' Okon added.

'Be safe,' Abel stated, and they split.

Abel and the group made it to the class block, just as one of Funke's security guys took a bullet in the head.

Osaz and Okon made for the entrance of the camp, their eyes scanning their surroundings for the sniper. Around them, some refugees lay dead; a lot of the living were still scampering. It was Okon who saw it first: a bright flash from the top of a tree, just before another IDP hit the ground. Okon signalled to Osaz, and they began their advance. They reckoned that a mop up squad was close by and were only waiting for a signal from the sniper. Osaz raised three fingers and began to count. On three, Okon shot in the air, causing some IDPs to run towards the sniper's position while Osaz shot at the sniper in the tree. There was a loud thud as the sniper fell from the tree.

'Sonofabitch,' Osaz spat.

Osaz made sure the sniper was dead while Okon took his gun. They were about to return to their comrades when they saw Danladi running towards them.

'Zey are coming! Zey are reinporcing!' He screamed.

Time check: 0730hrs.

Osaz and Okon began to run towards another class block. It was their only chance; there was no way they would make it back to their comrades before the onslaught. Danladi joined them in the class block next to the one Abel and the others were. They picked up Funke's PA on their way. She was hit, but the bullet had gone through. They patched her up and waited. They did not have to wait too long.

Intelligence had reached the base about the attack on the IDP camp. The General tried to find out if his men and his niece were safe, but no one could give him word. He ordered a chopper to be fuelled. The chopper had just left the base's airspace when an anti-aircraft missile hit it.

'Mayday, mayday, we've been hit. We are going down,' the helicopter pilot said before the chopper crashed. There were no survivors.

The information room got transmission from Sergeant Osaz; he radioed in that they needed help. The VIP was safe, but the insurgents were regrouping and coming at them in droves. They needed all the help they could get. The General was informed and he ordered some men to gear up and get help to their comrades. The men were engaged just outside their base. The insurgents were stationed close by and were determined to prevent any help from getting to the

IDP camp. The soldiers engaged the insurgents, but they soon beat a hasty retreat.

The General realised the insurgents were not interested in running over his base; all they wanted was to prevent a rescue mission. General Oluseyi geared up with his aide. Five soldiers saw their CO and asked what his plan was.

'We take the back of the camp and zero in on them. We attack them from the flank.'

'Yes, sir.'

The General and his men went out quietly and started making for the enemies' flank. The General's aide went to scout. He came back with intel about the anti-aircraft gun and an automatic machine gun on the ready. The guns were operated by a couple of men, while the others engaged the troops trying to leave the base.

The General asked three groups of two men each to separate and try to take out the men manning the guns so that they could have the advantage. The General's aide refused to leave his boss' side. The General maintained that he would be alright and right behind them. The General lay behind a sand dune when he heard movement atop him. An insurgent had come to relieve himself. The General covered his nose as he rolled away from the position. He was about to rise when he saw his aide's eyes open in fear. The General did not need to be told; he had been found out.

The General turned round in one swift movement and leapt at the insurgent, who was trying to hold his native trouser together with a rope. The General reached for the enemy's throat so he could strangle him. The other soldiers raised their guns, but the General shook his head from side to side, telling them not to shoot. He nodded for them to get to the insurgents handling the guns. The insurgent pulled out a knife and swung dangerously at the General. The

General stepped back and in one swift movement, advanced towards the insurgent's knife hand as it went back; at the right moment, he side-stepped causing the knife to slice the air past his side. He locked his assailant's arm and disarmed him. The knife fell to the ground, and the General head butted the insurgent on the chest, causing him to fall to the ground. The insurgent kicked the General behind the leg, causing him to fall on the sand. The insurgent lunged at his throat, and they rolled from side to side. The insurgent then tried to force the General's face on his faeces. The stench was bad. The General had had enough. The General hit the insurgent with his elbow and slammed his face in his faeces. The General stuck a knife into the insurgent's back.

The General lay on his back, panting. Then a figure stood over him. There was a wicked grin on this insurgent. 'I will be a hero for killing a General in this war,' he said, training his pistol on the General's face. 'Good night, General.'

Abel and his team watched as the insurgents moved in on their position in the school. Abel ordered his men not to let any insurgent within fifty metres of their position in the class block. By this time, they had all gone to the class on the first floor to get the aerial advantage. The doors were barricaded with tables and the windows were covered with boards. They were lucky to get some sandbags that the children in the IDP camp used to play 'monkey post' soccer. Osaz and Okon had done the same with Danladi's help. They waited for the enemy to get in range so they could make every bullet count. They knew help would not be on its way anytime soon. The base had radioed them. They were on their own.

Because of their aerial advantage, Lt. Col. Abel's men took down the insurgents in droves. The insurgents did not have a cover and did not seem interested in taking one. Abel saw a tango with an RPG and ordered Emeka to take him out. The insurgent with the RPG was shot in the head just as he squeezed the trigger. The force of the bullet pushed his hands up. The grenade went high in the air and came down amid his comrades. There was a loud explosion. The soldiers cheered. The insurgents were confused, and the soldiers took advantage. Many of the insurgents perished, and the rest scampered off.

'We need more aerial advantage,' Abel observed; facing Usman, he added, 'Usman, you are my best shot. Go to the top floor and take those bastards out when they regroup.'

'Yes, sir!' Usman said, running to the door.

Funke sat at a corner and watched the men plan their defence. She was gradually coming out of shock. She was surprised at the amount of chaos going on around her. She had never seen so much death and destruction before. She closed her eyes and cried. She jumped when she heard Emeka shout, 'They are coming back!'

In the other class, Osaz's eyes bulged as he saw the fire power the enemy were coming with; they had a rocket launcher on a truck and they were getting it in position. The launcher could fire twenty rounds in succession. 'We are so screwed,' muttered Osaz.

The General closed his eyes, thinking he would get a bullet in the head. A shot rang out, followed by a dull thud. The insurgent hit the ground at the same time the General's aide showed up.

'Are you okay, sir?'

'Yes, I am. Thank you.'

The General was helped up, and they moved towards the insurgents. They knew the gun shot would have attracted them. They had to take out the enemy fast.

The other men had engaged the insurgents shooting the gun. They had taken a good number of them out and were advancing towards the gun when a grenade rolled into their midst. 'Grenade!' one of the men screamed and they all dove out of range for cover. Immediately after the explosion, the insurgents saw no movement from the General and his men. There was still some smoke and they were waiting for it to clear. Just as the smoke began to clear, they heard shots; the General and his men shot through the smoke, killing all the insurgents. The General instructed a gunner to get behind the automatic machine gun. He fired away as the General and the men with him did their share of damage.

The General told two men to come with him; they needed to get to the IDP camp. They needed to get help to Abel and his team. The General instructed one of his men, a colonel to secure the camp and deploy more men to the IDP camp. They got into one of the vans the insurgents brought and drove in the direction of the IDP camp. The amount of fire power in the van was so much that the General began to wonder, for the umpteenth time, who the insurgent's sponsor was. Isaac manned the gun while the General's aide, Chidi drove.

In the IDP camp, Abel and his men faced a fresh dilemma. They were running out of ammo and ideas. They diverted most of their remaining ammunition to Usman and Okon who manned the high ground. Both men were expert marksmen who took out anyone who tried to get on the truck with the rocket launcher.

Danladi had an idea. He pushed the desk behind the door slightly and squeezed out of the class. He had been learning baseball and he was a very good thrower. He took his stance and swung a grenade as hard and as far as he could. The grenade fell on top of the launcher. The explosion was massive. The terrorists were in disarray and Danladi quickly ran into the open field to pick clips and guns off dead insurgents; Abel and Emeka closely followed him.

Back at the class, Abel wondered what the insurgents' next play was. What he saw made him squint, and then his eyes went wide.

The insurgents led three men out whose heads were covered with jute bags. The captives knelt, and their heads were uncovered. Abel and his men gasped.

The General and his men were fifteen minutes away from the IDP camp when they realised the enemy had flanked them on both sides. The enemy could not yet tell them apart because they were in one of the vans used to attack their base. But the General knew it was only a matter of time before they were found out. He ordered his aide to slow down; he also hoped Isaac had taken cover under the trampoline covering the weapons at the back of the van. Chidi made it look like the van was sputtering to a stop; he did not want it to be obvious they were slowing to a stop. The enemy bought it and drove past them in droves. But not all the vans drove past them. One van began to slow to a stop out of concern.

The van was parked behind theirs and three men came out; walking towards them. Isaac rose from under the covers and shot one of the men and the driver; the General also rolled out of the van and shot the other two. Chidi had his gun trained on the van, but did not shoot because there were two more vans approaching. They had no choice but to engage. Isaac manned the .50 calibre automatic on the van and fired away. The General and Chidi had their eyes on the other side; they could hear some of the vans that had moved ahead screech to a halt and begin their reverse journey.

The General ordered Chidi into the van and they moved the vehicle. They rode straight at the enemy, pretending that soldiers pursued them. Isaac gauged the distance and then rose in his fiery glory. Shells fell at his feet as he took out the drivers of the vans first before hitting their engines. The three vans somersaulted before blowing up — the General shot at some insurgents who had dived out of the vans. Chidi drove with one hand and shot a pistol with the other. The General knew the horde that would come upon them would be more than they could handle, so he ordered they ditched the vehicle and make it on foot. They could already see a billow of smoke and dust approaching from up ahead.

The General advised that they split up to have a better chance at survival. 'We rendezvous at…' he gave coordinates after consulting his map.

Chidi refused to leave his principal's side. 'Sir, my job is to stick with you.'

'Soldier, I am giving you a direct order. We. Are. To. Split. Up.' The General spoke, emphasising every word.

'Sir, I suggest we exchange uniforms so I can divert enemy attention. They would prefer to capture a high-ranking officer. It will give you time to plan and rescue our brothers.'

The General wanted to argue, but he knew the soldier was right; Isaac agreed, even though he did not voice his thoughts. In their haste to get to Abel and company, the General had not shed the insignia on his uniform.

'You are right. Evade and survive boys. We meet at the IDP camp in one hour, or the rendezvous point. If anyone does not get there five minutes after the time, we go on with the mission as planned.'

'Yes, sir!'

'Good luck, boys.'

The three captives kneeling in front of the insurgents were soldiers who had been declared missing for months. They had been declared first missing in action; then killed in action. Two of them were Emeka's friends from NMS, Zaria. He was furious and was shaking. Abel placed a hand on Emeka's shoulder.

'Stand down. Let us observe.'

They heard the first gun shot and one of the soldiers went down. It was a clean shot to the head. Usman and Okon shot simultaneously. The two insurgents they took down were replaced by another two. The second soldier was shot in the head too.

As the machete came down on the third, Usman and Okon shot. Emeka charged out of the sanctuary of cover like a mad man. Abel had no choice; he pulled up an RPG. Before he took the shot, he read the soldier's lips: 'Don't let me die like this. I deserve to go like a soldier and not an animal.'

The force of the explosion pushed Emeka back and he fell hard on the ground, tears in his eyes. Something gave in Emeka's head and he charged into the field to rescue his lost but found colleague. Abel ordered him to come back, but he did not. Despite the fact the other soldiers provided cover fire, Emeka got shot. His lifeless body ran a few more steps before he hit the ground. There would be no more wedding in two weeks.

To say Abel and his men's morale shrank as they heard the insurgents chant in victory was an understatement. Abel let out a few shots, taking out some insurgents. The men were so caught up in their sorrow that they did not hear Funke mumbling to herself. 'This is all my fault; I should not have come here. These men are dying because of me.' Then she decided to give herself up in a bid to save the soldiers. She left the group. It was when the soldiers heard the door bang shut that they realised someone had left the room.

'Shit!' Abel cursed as he saw the insurgents stop their chanting and face the VIP walking towards their position. It was quite a distance, but they were waiting patiently. She shouted in Arabic that the soldiers were not to come to harm once she gave herself up. One of the insurgents began to rub his crotch and narrow his eyes as he watched her come towards them.

The General could hear gun shots up ahead and he knew he was close. He heard some men in the woods; it seemed they were setting up camp. The insurgents were ready to wait as long as it took. The General pulled out his gun and then thought otherwise. He pulled out his jack knife and took a deep breath. He could make out three men. He waited for one of them to wander away from the group.

The General jumped out from behind a shrub and buried his knife in the lone insurgent's chest, with one palm clasped firmly over the dying man's mouth. He dragged the body further into the woods and hid it under some fallen branches. He walked back to the makeshift camp but noticed the two men were gone. He knew immediately that something was amiss. He crouched when he heard a twig snap; he still could not see anyone. He was trying to control his breathing. He was scared. He rose slowly and turned around. He was hit across the head with a branch. He passed out.

The General came to when water was thrown on his face. He found himself tied to a chair; he grunted as the insurgents began to punch him across the face. They looked at his stripes and were disappointed; they wanted a high-ranking officer, not a Sergeant. They unleashed their anger on the General's midsection and face. The General had begun to feel faint and feared he would pass out without being able to warn his boys.

The General knew he had to put up a fight to buy time for his boys to find him. So he rose as much as he could, still tied to the chair and charged at one of the insurgents. They fell in a heap. The General sank his teeth in the first insurgent's neck, making him writhe in pain. The other insurgent raced towards the duo and tried to get the General off his comrade. The General moved back suddenly and caught the other adversary's midsection with the chair. He crumbled to the ground. The General rolled off, the chair having broken; he was prepared to fight for his life. One of the terrorists pulled a gun.

'Die, bastard!' he said, his words dripping with hate.

There was a loud report.

Abel kept yelling for Funke to come back, but it seemed she had gone temporarily deaf. She was mumbling to herself as she made for the enemy. Rotimi went after her despite Abel's warning. He came out, guns blazing and turned on automatic gunfire on the insurgents. The vandals sought cover. Rotimi flung Funke over his shoulder and ran back to the building. He took a bullet in his leg and then two in the back for his troubles. He fell with his package, but used his body as a shield for Funke. He smiled at her with blood in his mouth. 'No one blames you,' he said, 'Now run.'

Funke was in tears as she tried to find where Rotimi was hurt. It was a serene moment as even the insurgents held their fire. She cradled the soldier's head to her bosom as he struggled for breath. One of the bullets had pierced a lung, and it was filling up with blood. 'I am sorry. I am so sorry,' she kept muttering with tears in her eyes.

Usman jumped out of the class and ran towards the fallen soldier. He had Funke stand behind him as he dragged his comrade with one hand; and with the other hand, he shot at the enemy. The others provided cover fire. The terrorists were distracted about this time as they heard gun shots from behind them. It was Usman that first saw it. 'RPG!' He shoved Funke away just before the explosion. When the smoke cleared, the Lieutenant had lost his legs and was in so much pain. He looked at the stub that was once his lower limb and started to cry.

Danladi had gone to get Funke while Abel dragged Usman across the grounds into the class. Abel was red with rage. Usman looked at where his feet used to be and began to scream; no one knew whether it was from the pain or the loss. The Lt. Col. put a tourniquet over the stubs, but he could not find any morphine. Abel gave Funke a mean look and went back to keeping watch. It was all those in the room could do to block out the grunting pain coming from the Lieutenant. Abel was shaking uncontrollably. He needed to make someone pay. Then they heard the gun shot. Usman had shot himself; he could not bear the pain anymore.

Sergeant Osaz tried reaching their base again. 'We need help, please,' his lips quivered. 'Please, somebody. Anybody!'

Abel sat there a while, staring at nothing. He had let his men down; he had lost three men, and now the rest were boxed in. They had no exfil plan. They were running low on ammo. They were there for the taking.

Like clockwork, Isaac and Chidi showed up just in time. Chidi shot the insurgent who was trying to kill his principal and Isaac shot the second. While Chidi circled round with his gun, Isaac went to the General's side to help him up. 'Sir, are you hit?'

'No, I'm not. I sure am glad to see you both.'

'Same here, sir.'

'The gunshot must have alerted the others; we need to fight, and hope backup comes soon. I believe they have some ammo in the makeshift tent.' the General stated.

The soldiers rounded up arms and advanced towards the enemy. They would cut off the enemy from behind. They had found RPGs and were not afraid to use it.

Abel stood up and began to make for the door. Danladi held him back. 'Aboki, no!' Abel looked into the boy's face. The boy muttered, 'It is not your fault, sir.'

Okon yelled, 'Tangos are advancing towards us, sir!' He fired some shots. 'We are running low on ammo.'

Abel shook his head to clear it and went back to the window. He shot at the advancing tangos and started praying for a miracle. Then, he heard the explosion from behind the enemy line; and another; and another. The explosions were followed by gun shots.

Abel charged out of the classroom and fired at the confused insurgents. 'Use the smoke for cover!' he screamed. The others charged out with him and fired away. The insurgents fell in their tens. When Abel used up his ammo, he pulled out his knife as an insurgent charged at him. Without slowing down, he weaved to the right and stabbed the insurgent in the back of the neck. He kept moving. His men raced alongside him; they needed to kill these bastards. They needed to make them pay for all the souls that had perished that day. Danladi ran beside Abel.

The General caught a bullet in his leg but kept on shooting. They were winning against the odds and that was good enough for him. He knew it was only a matter of time before the adrenaline cursing through his veins wore off and the pain would hit. Chidi never left his side again. He was determined to keep his principal alive.

When the smoke cleared, the soldiers looked around for any insurgent that was still breathing. It was while they were doing this that an insurgent raised his gun and shot twice at Abel. The bullets sailed across the grounds with Abel waiting for impact. It never happened; Danladi dove in front of him. The bullet hit Danladi in the chest and stomach.

Abel picked up a gun and shot the insurgent point blank.

'Bastard!' he spat.

'We need a medic!' Abel yelled as he heard their chopper land. He laid Danladi's head on his lap and tried to stop the bleeding. 'Look at me, Danladi!'

Abel shook the boy and shouted for a medic. The boy was already coughing out blood; the blood was black. The bullet had hit a lung.

The little boy smiled with difficulty and said, 'My debt is paid in full. Thank you, sir.'

'No!' Abel screamed. 'Look at me Danladi; you cannot die. I order you not to die!'

Danladi said, 'It is you who must not die, sir.' Cough. 'The country needs you to bring peace.' Cough. 'You are a good man, sir.' Danladi kept his smile as he raised his hand with much difficulty. He saluted the officer and then relaxed his hand, forever. Abel could not contain himself anymore; he wept. 'Thank you for your service,' he muttered. They had held off the enemy for ten hours. It was a miracle that anyone of them was still alive.

The bodies of the soldiers and Danladi were put in body bags. Abel stood over his dead men, with Okon and Osaz by his side. No words were said; they just stared at the bags. Abel walked towards Funke and her PA.

'Tell your father what happened here today. Tell him of the brave men who gave their lives to protect his daughter and this nation. Tell him!'

The two ladies kept crying as Abel spoke. He ended his statement with, 'They deserved better. Emeka's wedding was in two weeks; what do I tell his fiancée?' Abel walked away.

The soldiers watched the VIPs being airlifted out of the hot zone. The General refused to leave his men after he was patched up. Chidi supported him as he limped to Abel and his team. They were expecting another chopper to airlift the bodies and the soldiers still alive. 'I am so sorry, Abel,' the General said.

'It is not your fault, sir. This is what we all signed up for. It's just a pity it had to come to this.'

'You and your men still get to leave tomorrow,' the General said and patted Abel on the back.

IV

Two days later, Lt. Col. Abel walked into the hospital where his wife worked as a consultant urologist. He found the Matron and a nurse who knew him well, and they agreed to help him surprise his wife. He waited till she called for the next the patient.

Abel knocked on the door twice and pushed it open. He stood by the door and watched his wife; she was writing in a patient's folder.

'Please, have your seat,' she said without looking up. 'I'll be with you in a moment.'

Abel sat.

Finally, she looked into the card in front of her. 'Now, what seems to be the problem, Mr...,' she finally looked up. The words stuck in her throat. In their place came, first silence; then a scream; and then, tears. She rushed into his arms.

'Thank God, thank God. Thank you, Jesus,' Abel's wife said again and again.

The nurses came into the consulting room with smiles on their faces. The nurses joined her in her adulation. Abel waited for his wife to see her remaining patients. Then they went to pick their son in school.

In this moment of joyful reunion, Abel was glad to be with his beloved family. The joy was enough. He did not dampen the euphoria with the weight of his recent experience in the theatre of death. He would wait for two days before telling her about Danladi, the lad who had jumped in front of a bullet and died in his place; he would tell her how they had draped a flag on his makeshift coffin and given him a twenty-one-gun salute. He would tell her about Usman, who had lost both legs in battle and shot himself in the head because he could not bear living as a disabled person. He would tell her about the VIP whose naiveté took several lives including Rotimi's. He would tell her that there would be no wedding for Emeka and that he had to don his ceremonial uniform to break the news of death in the face of joyful preparation. That some of his men, whom she had known, would never come home.

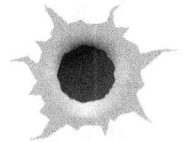

NEXT MINUTE

I

It was Sunday morning and Dr Akpan and his family of five were about to go to church. Everyone was getting into the car when Edidiong, the eldest child, suddenly developed a running stomach and ran into the toilet. Dr Akpan hated getting anywhere late. As a surgeon, he knew from experience that every minute counted and extended this ethic to every aspect of his life. He would not wait for Edidiong, he stated. Edidiong asked them to go ahead; he would go for the next service of the day.

Immediately the car pulled out of the house, Edidiong went to the sitting room and turned on the television. He had missed an episode of *Tinsel* and wanted to watch the repeat broadcast which was shown every Sunday morning.

Dr Akpan drove to church singing choruses with his family. His daughter, Cynthia saw a rundown Peugot504 parked at the side of the road. The driver had a frustrated look to him. Dr Akpan parked beside him and spoke in fluent Hausa, 'Good morning. What is wrong with your vehicle?'

The good-looking Hausa man smiled and explained that one of the tyres had gone flat and he did not have a spare. So, Dr Akpan offered an old tyre from his trunk. The man was grateful and waved as they drove off. 'Na gode. Thank you.'

'Darling,' Mrs Akpan called, 'Did you notice he did not open his boot to get his jack and other tools until we left?'

'Yes; but maybe he was ashamed. Did you see that car? It's ancient,' Dr Akpan replied.

'His action just looked suspicious to me; that's all.'

'My analyst wife, not everything in this world is complicated. I don't think there was anything to it.'

At the church, the service was exhilarating. The church was packed full because it was the third service. As the service ended and church members were coming out, a rundown Peugot 504 sped in. Dr Akpan recognised it as the same car with the same good-looking man he had helped that morning. 'What's the hurry,' he thought, 'and why doesn't he stop?'

The man behind the wheel of the 504 was chanting the takbir as the car rammed into some parked cars. Suddenly, there was a deafening bang. The church had been hit by a suicide bomber.

Sergeant Femi Adele was in the hospital when his phone rang. He was expecting his first child, and his wife had been wheeled into the delivery room. His team leader in the anti-bomb squad was at the end of the line. Quickly, Femi informed one of the nurses to please let his wife know that he had been summoned at work.

At the bomb site, Femi was shocked at the extent of the damage. He, like everyone present, believed that the church building was felled by a very powerful bomb. He could also hear people blaming Boko Haram for the mayhem. Femi and his team started combing the crash site and its environments for any more explosives.

Emergency management officials were being shouted at because their leader said they had only counted ten bodies.

'What rubbish is this one saying?' said someone.

'Fifty people have been taken to the mortuary!' said another.

The soldiers and police men had their work cut out for them.

After Edidiong finished watching *Tinsel,* he took a bike to the church. On his way, he noticed the fire service and members of other emergency services speeding past. He wondered what had happened and went his way to the church.

When Edidiong got to the church, the sight that greeted his eyes was one that he had only ever seen in movies. The whole place was a mixture of rubble, burnt cars, crying people and charred corpses. Somehow, the first thing that crossed his mind was that he thanked God he had stayed back at home or he, too, would have been blown to bits.

Edidiong suddenly recognised his father's Toyota Avensis. It's windscreen was smashed in and the rest of the car was hidden under another car that had obviously flipped and landed on top of it. Panic seized him. 'Where is my family?' he asked.

As if to answer his question, Edidiong saw his mother and sisters' remains wheeled inside an ambulance. He screamed after them, but he was held back. It was where he stood shedding tears and wondering about his father that he saw a suspicious looking back pack and called the attention of the bomb squad.

Sergeant Femi and a soldier knelt beside the bag and began their assessment. While the soldier worked, a member of the squad told Femi, 'Word from the hospital; your wife has given birth to a bouncing baby boy. They are both doing well.' Sergeant Femi smiled. The next minute; there was an explosion. The bomb in the backpack had been detonated by a remote trigger.

II

Kunle's plane taxied to a halt at the airport in Kano. He had flown in from America via Amsterdam with a brief stopover in Lagos, before coming to Kano. Kunle Pierce was a CIA intelligence officer. He was Sergeant Femi Adele's friend and brother-in-law.

Kunle consoled his sister and made the funeral arrangements. Lucky for him, he was given some time off and asked to lay low after a successful clandestine operation in the Middle-East. Every time he looked at his nephew, doomed to grow up without his father, Kunle's determination grew. Somebody had to pay.

Kunle began studying reports from the CIA and SSS. He hoped to find a pattern so he could figure out how the terrorists operated. He would go to every venue of bombings the Boko Haram sect claimed responsibility for.

Kunle was driving into town one Wednesday afternoon when he heard the explosion. He saw people running and he asked them what happened. A police station had been bombed. He drove into the area where the police station was. He ran into one of the banks and talked to the security guards on duty. In five minutes, he issued instructions to the Manager of the bank, and in another five minutes, all the banks in the area were informed. Kunle knew the sect thrived on diversion. It was possible that the explosion at the police station was a diversion so that the vandals could bomb the banks, and, perhaps, loot their vaults.

He sat in his car, watching for anyone who looked out of place. His wait paid off; he saw a bearded man with a back pack, mumbling. He looked round and noticed that the man kept looking back to a particular car.

Kunle moved cautiously towards the car. He hoped he could save the people in the bank. There were three men in the car. They did nothing to hide their rifles. Kunle was almost by the car when suddenly the door opened. Shit!

Kunle pulled out his side arm and moved on. One of the men, who Kunle suspected was from one of the neighbouring Islamic countries pointed at him. The others raised their rifles and fired at him. Kunle jumped into an open door by his side. Luckily for him, his assailants were bad shots. It was obvious that the only thing they knew about the guns they were handling was to pull the trigger.

Kunle took one of the men out. He changed his cartridge clip and noticed the bomber had stopped. Apparently he was confused. He began to run towards the car, as he saw another of his comrades go down. The third man in the car faced the bomber, yelling at him in Arabic to go back.

Kunle ran out shooting, forcing the third man to move towards the bomber. When the two men met in the middle of the road, Kunle shot the bomb. Boom, there was a loud bang. Kunle was thrown back.

Kunle got to his feet and shook his head to regain focus. People ran to the scene from all directions; a siren started wailing in the distance. Some soldiers and a few policemen cordoned off the area. After receiving the gratitude of the bankers, Kunle was taken into custody to be debriefed.

Kunle gave the Joint Task Force (JTF) commander his analysis of the sect's modus operandi. They were grateful for his help and promised to keep his identity secret, as he requested. Kunle promised to keep in touch, and went home to his sister.

The next Sunday, a man opened fire on worshippers coming out of a worship service. No bomb was used. No one claimed responsibility. No arrests were made. Nothing, only splotches of crimson on whitewashed wall; dead bodies and grieving relatives.

Kunle decided to take his sister out for lunch. She had not been out of the house since Femi's death. Her grief found no outlet because Femi had no grave. There was no place to grieve, no grave where she could go to speak with her late husband. Her pain was inward and it had started to eat her up. They drove around the ancient walls of Kano before making their way to Cilantro Restaurants and Lounge on Sultan road. He had heard that it was the best restaurant in Kano. He hoped the ambience of the place would lighten her mood. His sister's baby, oblivious of the state of affairs, was in a pram. Kunle tried to make his sister laugh. 'You shouldn't feel guilty for being happy, you know,' he said, when he noted Kemi wearing a pained look.

'But Femi is dead,' she protested.

'And it's not your fault. If a bunch of misguided fundamentalists decide to behave like mad people, you shouldn't hold yourself responsible.'

'But...,' Kemi wasn't allowed to finish.

'It's not your fault. Junior needs you to be happy; I want you to be happy.' Kunle held his sister's hands across the table, looking her in the eye.

Across the road, a bearded man spoke into his cell phone, 'They are still in the restaurant.'

'Have you fixed it?' the voice on the other end asked.

'Yes.'

'Make sure everything goes without a hitch.'

'Yes.'

The line went dead.

Kunle, Kemi and Junior made their way to their car. Kunle was about to open the door when the key dropped. He was still speaking to Kemi when he knelt to pick the key. He froze as he saw a familiar package under the car. It had a blinking red light.

'Get away from the car,' Kunle shouted.

When he looked up, his heart stopped.

A clean shaven man stood, holding Kemi from behind. The man had a gun to her back. Kemi held her baby to her chest and whimpered. The baby started to cry. The clean shaven man smiled a gold toothed smile.

'Let her go and I'll let you live,' Kunle said, his gun drawn.

The man laughed. 'Who said I am afraid to die?' He spoke to Kemi with a wicked smile. 'Now, move.'

The man moved with his hostages and Kunle started to follow.

A car engine revved and Kunle looked to his side. An unmarked car was speeding his way. He turned towards it and fired two shots from his Colt to deter the driver. The driver did not stop; Kunle got hit by the car. The car only stopped after it crashed into a parked bus. Kunle landed on his back. From his position on the floor, he watched his sister and nephew pushed into the van. He stretched his hand and mouthed, 'No.' He tried to memorise the license plate as he lapsed into unconsciousness.

Kunle came to some hours later and was told the situation with his car had been contained. There was no word of his sister or her child.

'I'm sorry. We can only assume they are...,' the detective couldn't bring himself to complete the statement.

A doctor came in with charts and Kunle asked, 'When can I leave?'

'In two days. You are lucky you sustained no major injuries, but we want to observe you in case of a concussion.'

'Thanks doc, but I need to go. My sister is in danger and I have to save her,' Kunle said.

'You can't leave today. We need to observe you,' the doctor replied.

Kunle sat up in bed and made to get off the bed, to the doctor's chagrin. The doctor had just stepped up to him when a loud explosion rocked the hospital. The hospital had been hit by a bomb.

III

Kemi looked around the bare room she was locked in and sobbed. She prayed Kunle was alright. She had heard her abductors saying Kunle had been taken to the hospital by passers-by. She fingered a chip fit on the button of her jeans. It was a gift Kunle had given her to make her feel safe whenever he was not around. He had instructed her to carry it everywhere. She hoped Kunle was alive. She held her son and prayed.

The door to the room opened two hours later. The same man who initiated her abduction came in dressed in a clean white Arabian thobe robe and black trousers. He fiddled with cufflinks as he spoke. 'Your brother is dead. We bombed the hospital where they kept him. No one is coming to get you. They are all dead!'

Kemi caught her breath and began to sob.

'Don't worry,' her abductor smiled and went on. 'You and your baby will soon join him. You will go with the suicide team in two days, insha Allah.'

The door closed and Kemi started to cry afresh. Junior soon joined her.

Kemi woke with a start. She heard the door to the room that housed her open slowly. The light from the passage streamed in, she made out the outline of a man. Her body became tense as the man knelt over her. His hand touched her right breast. She was about to be raped. With all the strength she had left, she swung in the dark. She connected with her assailant's head and heard a grunt. She swung again, but hit nothing. She got to her feet as the light came on.

Kemi stopped fighting and pulled her polo shirt over her head; and was undoing her jeans.

'Make it quick,' she said.

'What? What are you doing?' her assailant asked, his Hausa accent not too obvious.

'You want to fuck me, don't you?' she stated, and added, 'Just be gentle is all I ask. You can see I've just had a baby.'

'No. Please put your clothes back on,' the man said, and turned his back.

Kemi was shocked, then relieved. She had not had a plan, but she had figured there was no use fighting a man who had a gun and hastening her own death. She put her clothes back on and asked:

'So what do you want? You were groping at my breast!'

'That was a mistake, I swear to God,' the man replied, and then he added, 'I've come to get you out. I don't support what my uncle does.'

'Hamisu, what are you doing there?' asked a guard who happened to pass by as the door opened. Hamisu stepped out and shut the door behind him.

'Didn't you see the woman? Wallahi that woman is fine!'

Ahmed laughed stupidly. 'Yes, she is,' he said, and then lowering his voice added, 'I masturbated earlier this evening with her body on my mind.'

'You see. I just had to..., you know. Her full breast, tiny waist, nice hips and round nyash. Ahmed her body was so soft and when I got into her, it felt like...' Hamisu groaned.

He noticed the bulge forming in Ahmed's trouser. Ahmed too wanted a taste.

Ahmed walked into the dark room and Hamisu struck him at the back of the head. He passed out. Hamisu led Kemi out and told her to keep the baby quiet. Thankfully, Junior was fast asleep. They had made it down the flight of stairs without being seen. The entrance door was in sight. It looked like they might escape without a hitch.

The door opened and in came two armed guards. Kemi hid behind a settee and prayed silently. She heard the three men exchange pleasantries. The two guards had got to the stairs when junior woke up and began to cry. Without thinking, Hamisu pulled out his gun and shot the two guards. He had no silencer.

The house came alive and Hamisu engaged the other guards with the assault rifle of the dead guards. He was overwhelmed and held Kemi to him. Kemi was scared. There was a big blast.

IV

Kunle Pierce got out from under the rubble. He discovered a few people who had survived the blast. The detective and doctor were not so lucky. Looking around him, his resolve to make those responsible pay heightened.

He got home and changed into combat trousers and a black tee shirt. He topped it with a black jacket and packed his gun and stash of ammunition into his trousers' many pockets. He heard a beeping sound coming from his GPS device. Kemi was alive and transmitting her location. He was taking the war to 'the bastards.'

Hamisu and Kemi realised the shooting had stopped. They made their way through the smoke and got to the door. A gun was in their face.

'One false move and you're toast,' the voice behind the gun said.

Kemi could have fainted for joy. 'Kunle, you're alive!'

Kunle held unto his sister, but his gun was trained on Hamisu. 'Who the hell are you?' he asked.

It was Kemi who replied. 'He rescued me,' then facing Hamisu, 'I didn't quite get your name.'

'My name is Hamisu.'

A gun shot rang out.

Hamisu fell to the ground while Kunle shot in the direction of the gun fire. Kemi was on her knees beside the gasping Hamisu. Junior began to cry again. 'Please don't die,' she sobbed.

Kunle went further into the building. Kemi heard a couple of rounds go off. She said a quiet prayer for her brother; she tried to make Junior stop crying.

Kunle came back and looked at Hamisu. The dying man beckoned him to come closer. Hamisu held unto Kunle and whispered in his ear. Kunle felt Hamisu's hand go limp as he took his last breath. Kemi burst into fresh tears as she pleaded with her brother to revive her saviour. There was nothing he could do. It was time to leave.

Kunle felt certain that the police and army had been compromised. He also knew he had to get his sister and her baby out of the area. He should have gone to the police or army with the information Hamisu gave, but he knew he could be endangering his own life. Hamisu had given names and addresses of bomb factories and key members of Boko Haram. Kunle knew that if he gave the information to the police and the army, nothing would come of it. Apart from being compromised, Nigeria's security operations were often loud. They could not carry out one covert operation without the news hinting at it first.

As if to prove Kunle right, the army began a series of televised raids on suspected bomb factories in the remote areas in the state. Kunle waited and watched. Some of the raids were so close to some of the places where Hamisu had told him about and he knew that those factories would soon disappear.

Around this time, Kunle was invited by the police and asked if he had any information. He was told to report any unusual events to the police. Kunle answered in the affirmative. He had just confirmed that there was a mole in the police force who wanted to know what he knew. He was even told by the police that he was being watched. Kunle knew he had to initiate his own covert operation, Operation Shadow Walker. First, he moved his sister and her baby out of harm's way. He sent her to Lagos.

Hamisu had given him names of three men who sponsored the

terrorists. All of them were highly placed government officials: two of them were serving senators.

A week later, the three men whose names Hamisu had given Kunle raised an alarm that their parents had been kidnapped. A video on the internet showed Boko Haram claiming responsibility for the kidnapping. The video caused rancour among the sect's ranks as they swore to their sponsors that they had no hand in the kidnappings. So, while the senators and security officials foamed at the mouth on TV, promising that they would 'leave no stone unturned' until they secured the senior citizens, Boko Haram was contacting all its cells and branches to know and see who performed the unauthorised kidnapping. The senators asked their beneficiaries to find their parents or get no funds.

V

An interdenominational crusade was holding in an open field in Abuja. The gathering wanted to pray for peace. The field was filled beyond capacity. Everyone seemed to agree that only God, not security operatives, could stop the bloodshed. So, they came to beseech God, while they were guarded by anti-riot policemen.

Kunle watched from a safe distance as a Honda Civic approached the crusade ground. He looked to his side and pushed a button.

A minivan blocked the path of the Honda Civic. The driver of the Honda Civic would not be deterred and hit the gas. The car sped on and just before impact, the door opened to reveal the bewildered parents of the sect's benefactors who were kidnapped. They were all tied together. The next minute, there was an explosion.

The preacher leading the crusade was the first to bolt. The congregation soon joined. Lots of people sustained injuries; twenty people died due to the ensuing stampede and not the bomb.

The three sponsors got parcels the next day. It was a video showing how their parents were tied up and put into the car. The sponsors watched in horror as their parents were blown to bits. Two of them suffered a heart attack. They died two days later.

The sect members were angry and claimed that external powers had a hand in the last attack. The day after the two men were buried, the UN building in Abuja was bombed. The whole world stood in shock.

The surviving senator was picked up and questioned about having ties with the Boko Haram sect. He denied the allegations and said it was impossible for him, a patriotic citizen who served the masses, to be in cahoots with terrorists. Kunle was sick to his stomach. He decided to teach the senator a lesson.

Kunle decided to lay low for some time. He'd decided against just killing people. Terrorism and insurgency in any country is a hydra-headed monster, and Nigeria was not exempt.

Kunle knew that for everyone he killed, someone else took their place. So, he decided that he would do something definitive and stem the tide of violence. He had two weeks before the end of his leave. He relocated his sister and her child to the United States, and set about his plan.

VI

The guest house was in the more quiet areas of Abuja, and can be used for many things. It could be a getaway for a quick short rest, the venue for an exclusive party or the site for some shenanigans. The surviving senator's most trusted aide had booked a room under an alias, so no one could trace the room to the Senator. The Senator liked little girls, so a pubescent girl had been selected and was waiting in the room.

The Senator was not one to waste time. Immediately the door closed, he took off his 'agbada' and began to undo his trouser. Kunle watched from the wardrobe.

The girl, a pro at her game, grabbed the senator and sucked on his member; licking his testicles and rolling them in her hands. The senator moaned and gripped the sheets. After a while, he told the girl to bend over and rammed into her from behind. The girl, with her nipples pointing to the floor, begged and cried and laughed and praised the senator in turn. Kunle watched the travesty and almost threw up. He thought the man wouldn't stop. Finally, the senator fell limp beside the girl and they both fell asleep.

When Senator Agada came to, he found himself in a dark room, tied to a chair.

'Welcome back Senator,' a metallic voice said.

'Where am I? Who are you? What do you want? Why am I here?' the Senator quizzed.

'One at a time, Senator. I see you are eager to talk. I may answer your questions, but first, you have to answer some of mine,' the metallic voice said.

The Senator was silent.

'By your silence, I take it you are ready!'

'I am not ready for anything. Untie me now.'

'Senator, do you finance the activities of the Boko Haram sect?'

'What sort of question is that? The government absolved me. If you are SSS, you should know; I want to speak to your superiors!'

'I don't work for the government. Answer the question, truth-fully!' the metallic voice said.

The Senator could detect a warning in the tone. 'No, I won't!'

A screen came on and the Senator watched the bombing of a church.

'Why are you showing me this?'

The pictures changed and the Senator watched the account of the death of his parents, alongside the parents of the other two. He screamed.

'I ask you again; do you finance Boko Haram?'

'You bastard! You will pay. Do you know who I am? I am a serv-ing Senator of the Federal Republic of Nigeria. You are finished; I will destroy you...' the threats went on.

'Shut up!' the metallic voice bellowed.

'Let's try a little motivation,' the metallic voice said. The picture changed to that of the Senator ramming away at a prepubescent girl in a bare hotel room.

The senator scoffed. 'How did you get this?'

'Same way I got this,' the metallic voice said, and the picture changed. Senator Agada almost died of shock. His wife and children were tied and gagged.

'Please,' Senator Agada said. 'What do you want? Please don't hurt my family.'

'Answer my questions truthfully!'

The Senator sang like a canary.

'What do you want me to do? I'll do anything,' the Senator said.

'First, you will resign your position as a Senator,' the voice said.

'I agree. Please, just don't hurt my family,' the tired Senator re-plied.

'Even though I know the sect will spring up again, I need names; and where I can find them.'

The Senator hesitated at first, but then told everything he knew. Soon, he was coughing. He was knocked out by gas seeping into the room.

The Senator came to in a car and looked round. He recognised the area and began to drive. As Kunle expected, he drove to a large house in a secluded area of Abuja. Hamisu had told him of this house, it was the operational headquarters of Boko-Haram in Abuja.

Kunle had bugged Senator Agada without his knowledge. So, he was able to listen to their conversation. An emergency meeting was called. Kunle settled down to listen to their conversation.

What Senator Agada and those in the meeting did not know was that they were live on radio and over the internet. When Senator Agada got home that night, he was appalled to see himself on CNN and BBC, confessing to financing Boko-Haram and mentioning names of other sponsors.

In the end, the President declared a state of Emergency in three states in Northern Nigeria and had all the men named in the video arrested.

Back in the United States, Kunle knew it was not going to be an easy case to sweep under the carpet. The world had proof and was watching; the International Court of Justice had proof and was watching. Kunle himself had proof, perhaps more than the whole world. He, too, was watching.

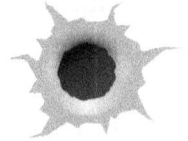

AJUWAYA– THE FIGHTING CORPS

I

After a long day at the polls, polling unit officers started to count votes in the presence of party agents and voters who hadn't gone home. At the end of the count, the people returned to their homes. They had performed their civic duty; they had seen the process through and they left with mixed reactions.

'I knew President Jonathan would win this place.'

'Walahi, they rigged the election. The General should have won!'

'Haba, mana. We all saw the count. Those corpers tried, gaskiya. Let's hope they don't do the rigging up up.'

'Amin'

'Sai Gobe'

'Allah Kiyaye'

The corps members heard this conversation shouted by two men. They had no stake in the matter, except their pay as INEC ad-hoc staff so they said nothing. As they packed their gear, they were glad there was no violence. Days to the National Assembly polls, they had lost some colleagues to a bomb blast in Suleja. The victims were at the INEC office to check their posting when the IEDs exploded. Many of the wounded were still in the hospital.

When the corps members got to their lodge that night, they checked in with their other colleagues and compared notes.

'Papa, we have one more election to go, and we're done,' Ochuko told his fellowship leader.

'Yeah; I pray it goes well. These people can be funny when things don't go their way,' Papa Kenny replied.

'Nothing will happen, Papa. The process was free and fair; they all witnessed it.'

'I hope they agree with you.'

That night, all the corps members in the lodge gathered to thank God for their safety and pray for the safety of other corps members in the country. They asked God to keep them safe and bring lasting peace to the country. They also asked God to bring healing to the wounded in the hospital and succour to the families of those who had died. While Papa Kenny prayed, the words his pastor said just before the election came to his mind. 'The peace of the North has expired,' the pastor had said.

'Amen,' all the corpers responded as Papa Kenny rounded off the prayer.

Since the day Ade started teaching at the Government Girls Secondary School in Birin Kudu, he set his eyes on Halima: the light-skinned, buxom girl who always kept to herself. It seemed the girl had taken a liking to him too. So, he bided his time and they were soon talking and meeting regularly after school.

Ade applied his body spray and anti-perspirant. He took another look in the mirror, slipped his NYSC cap in his back pocket and checked his wallet for his ID card and he was done. He grabbed his phone and headed out. He hoped to get lucky today.

They were talking over a drink, when Halima suggested they get a room.

'A room?' Ade said, raising his brow and grinning.

Halima cocked her head to one side and said nothing. Ade began to shake in excited anticipation. He went to the counter and paid for a room. In a few minutes, the room was prepared and they were shown in. The door had hardly closed before they grabbed each other. As their lips locked and their bodies became one; Ade thanked his luck. Halima cried afterwards, saying she didn't want to marry the Alhaji she had been betrothed to since she was little. Ade was trying to calm her, when he heard noise coming from outside. It seemed many people were speaking in rapid Hausa at the same time. Then they heard a crash.

Ade jumped out of the bed but Halima held him back telling him not to go.

'I have to see what's happening,' Ade said.

'It's a riot. They are saying that the General was robbed during the election,' Halima said. She listened some more, then turned to Ade; her eyes widened in fear. 'They say, you corpers rigged the election for President Jonathan; that he gave you people presidential gifts. They say you will all pay with your lives!'

Ade began to sweat. There was a knock on the door. Ade hid inside the wardrobe. Halima wore her clothes and opened the door.

'Where is za ajuwaya who came with you?' shouted the man at the door.

'Ajuwaya? Nobody came with me,' Halima replied calmly.

'The owner of this hotel said, you came here with one Kopa to fuck yourselves.'

'Kai, how dare you? Alhaji Tanko will hear this; he was the one who asked me to meet him here!' she lied.

'Okay; call him!' one of the men handed her a phone.

Halima looked round; she saw the anger and violence in the eyes of the men at the door.

'Go ahead, call him!'

Halima's hands shook as she collected the phone. She hit the buttons slowly, and then stopped.

'Be fast about it, we don't have time.'

Halima looked into the face of the leader of the mob. 'So, you want me to call Alhaji because you are accusing me? Show me the manager who told you I brought a corper here. I want to show him to Alhaji when he comes.'

Suddenly, there was shouting outside; a mob was pursuing a corps member.

'Bura ubanka! Shege banza!' The men at Halima's door ran out to the crowd. Their leader looked at Halima, 'I am watching you,' he said.

Halima locked the door and was shaking.

'Are they gone?' Ade asked, coming out from the wardrobe.

'They will come back,' Halima said.

'Let's find another room and hide,' Ade said. 'We can lock ourselves in. That way, they won't find us.'

'Wayo, wayo Allah. Aaah, wayo!' they heard moans from another room.

Ade peeped through the keyhole; he saw Ochuko, a fellow corps member and NCCF Bible Study Coordinator in the room with another girl. He knocked. The noise stopped.

Ochuko could have died of shock when Ade walked in, followed by Halima.

'Ade, what da...' he started.

'Shut up. We are in danger,' Ade said, closing the door, and turned the lock. After Ochuko and the lady got dressed, Ade briefed him on their situation.

'Ah, Jesus! But we prayed.'

Ade looked at Ochuko; he said nothing.

They heard some noise. 'They are coming back,' Halima said.

'I can talk to them,' the other girl, Zainab offered.

'No!' Ochuko said.

'That won't work,' Halima said, 'I tried it before.'

They heard a door kicked open.

'Oh my God!' Ade said silently, 'They are in our room.'

II

Papa Kenny had gone to town to check his mail. He was just leaving when two of his students ran to meet him. The two boys were panting, and he was trying to calm them down when three more students came running to him. Without saying a word, the boys dragged Papa Kenny into the bush.

'Mallam, run!'

'What is it?' Papa Kenny asked.

'Mallam, there is a riot. They are killing corpers!'

'What? Why? Who?'

'Mallam. Me, I don't know. But they are plenty that are killing them. They are singing. They are saying you collect money for election. That they thief the General's vote!'

'Ah!' Papa Kenny exclaimed. 'What should I do?'

'Follow us,' one of the boys said; it was Badaru. 'We know shortcut. But you must hurry. Gudu.'

Papa Kenny ran. He didn't think whether he trusted the boys or not. He did not know where they were headed, and he did not care. He just moved with the wind, and hoped that it would carry him to safety.

Suddenly, the boys came to a halt. There was a mob chasing some corps members. The boys turned. 'Mallam Papa, follow us. Gudu, gudu,' they told Papa Kenny. But Papa Kenny stood frozen, in fear.

'Mallam, let's go!' Badaru called. When Papa Kenny did not answer, the boys dragged him into a compound and told him to hide inside an outhouse.

In the small room, Papa Kenny peeped through a crack and saw that eight corps members had been caught. The ladies among them were taken aside and forced to watch as the mob lynched their colleagues.

'Nama, nama!' the mob yelled, as they macheted the corps members to their deaths. Papa Kenny gasped, but did nothing. He could not risk being caught.

After killing the male corps members, some of the vagrants undid their trousers. Their uncircumcised penises tumbled out, hard as a rock. The ladies whimpered but did not scream because of the weapons.

'Dan Allah!' they pleaded, as the boys closed in. But the boys were unmoved by their pleas. One by one, the boys raped the girls till they passed out.

Papa Kenny felt a hand on his shoulder. In one swift movement, he swung round and raised his fist to land a blow; he didn't. It was a female corps member.

'I'm sorry. How did you get here?' he asked, whispering.

'I scaled over the fence. They are killing us,' she said, and began to sob.

'Shh, shh, don't make a noise. They must not know we are in here. If they find us, we are dead,' Papa Kenny said, and the girl nodded. 'Please, what is your name?'

'Nkechi'

'Kenny...'

'I know who you are, Papa Kenny'

'We have to be strong now. We are still in danger,' he stated, holding her by her shoulders. She nodded.

Nkechi looked through another hole in the wall and saw the comatose female corps members being macheted to their deaths. Nkechi opened her mouth to scream but Papa Kenny clasped his hand over her mouth. Papa Kenny's students stood there stone faced, as they watched their people killing the helpless corps members.

As Papa Kenny peeped, he saw that a member of the mob was walking towards the outhouse. He turned and apprised every one of the situation. He looked to the boys and asked what he should do. The boys told Papa Kenny to be silent, and went out. They chased each other, laughing till they got close to the mob.

'Barka da rana,' the boys greeted the mob.

'Lahiya lau.'

They asked them if there was anyone else in the outhouse with them.

'No,' they replied, saying it was their mother's outhouse and she was resting. The mob's leader looked at them and asked the group to turn back. Suddenly, one of them turned and said he saw a female corper around the outhouse.

'Ne shi gaskiya? Is this true?' the leader of the mob asked.

'Babu shi ne karya; Wallahi. No, it is a lie.' The boys swore.

The leader of the mob, on hearing the boys deny and swear in God's name started to leave.

'Then let's check the compound,' another mobster said.

'Shiga,' the boys said, and the mob advanced towards the house with machetes, bottles and knives. Nkechi began to piss on herself.

Halima and Zainab looked at each other in the motel room. Ochuko and Ade stood there, cowering behind the door.

'Hide under the bed!' Zainab ordered, but Ade thought otherwise.

'Babu,' Halima said, 'the wardrobe will be better.'

'Then, be quick about it,' Zainab said, 'We will lock you in. Don't make any noise; don't even cough.'

Ochuko and Ade entered into the wardrobe as the ladies began to strip. Zainab locked the corps members in. The door jerked open. Halima and Zainab grabbed their clothes about them.

'Kai, ba shiga!' Zainab shouted.

The leader of the mob ran back followed by his cronies. He tried to apologise, but Zainab waved him away.

Zainab made sure the mob was gone before opening the wardrobe door.

'Mun gode. Thank you.' Ade said.

'What did you do?' Ochuko asked, surprised.

'We pretended that we were in the middle of dressing up, and that we had veils. So they back-tracked and ran away,' Zainab answered.

Ade and Ochuko were grateful for Zainab's genius. Each man went to his girl, and it was then Ade noticed Halima was shaking; he held her.

Zainab was more composed. She lay down on the bed and put her head on Ochuko's lap, staring into space. Suddenly, she sprang up, 'You have to go!'

'What?' Ade said; Halima stopped shaking and looked up questioningly.

'You need to get to your lodge,' Zainab said, 'You are not safe here'

Ade decided to call Papa Kenny. Maybe his fellowship leader could bring the cavalry.

The boys hoped Papa Kenny would take the initiative and run before they led the mob to the outhouse. Papa Kenny looked through the crack in the wall and saw that the vandals were approaching the house. He quickly grabbed Nkechi and bolted out of the house. The mob saw and gave chase. The duo went in between some huts, crashing into barns and stores.

'I'm getting tired,' Nkechi panted, as she ran.

Papa Kenny looked to his watch, 'We just have to evade them for ten more minutes!'

'How do you mean?' she asked, not slowing down.

'It will soon be time for them to pray; there will be less of them on the streets then.' They took a turn, and saw a staff in their school. She signalled to them to go into a hut by their side.

'Go!' Papa Kenny pushed Nkechi in the direction of the hut.

'What?' she asked, in shock.

'Someone has to keep them busy or they'll search everywhere. Now go!' he ordered, slowing down a bit. He had two minutes to outrun the mob.

The mob saw him jump over the fence and went after him. He navigated in between some buildings.

'Allah akbar, Allah ha ha hahaha akbar...' the muezzin called for prayer.

When Papa Kenny got into the hut, he saw that Nkechi had company; four other corps members were hiding with her.

'We've got about fifteen minutes to get back to our lodge' Papa Kenny said.

'I am tired,' Nkechi stated.

'Look, if we can get to the lodge, we will be safe. Just promise me you will do your best to keep up. Follow me closely and don't stop for any reason, okay.'

'Okay,' Nkechi answered.

'Let's go.'

Papa Kenny and his group made it to the corpers' lodge. As they got into the compound, Nkechi fell to the ground and started crying. One of the sisters offered her water. Papa Kenny's phone rang. He picked it.

'Hello...hello, Ade. Ah...are you alone? Who is with you? Ehen? Fadama? That's far out. You and Ochuko should stay put o...I know, but you can't make it back in such a short time...Try to survive. We will come and get you at night...Okay...Okay. But keep your phone on...Yes, yes. No, don't let it ring out; put it on vibration...We need to know where you are when we come get you...Alright, alright...Be calm. It is well.' Papa Kenny cut the call. Papa Kenny watched other corps members arrive. Most of them were injured, and had barely escaped with their lives.

Papa Kenny and the CLO called all the corps members in their lodge. The place was full because all the corps members who were in the area ran to the closest lodge. The CLO addressed the corps members.

'Okay guys, we have to protect ourselves. Our lives are at risk. I am happy we have weapons and tactical training. As you all know, this lodge like other lodges has an armoury. All of us will get weapons and defend ourselves. We have only one objective, guys. And it is to make sure that you and the person next to you stay alive. We must do everything possible to make sure that these vandals don't get anywhere near our lodge. Some of our ladies will be working with the medical team to treat the injured. Today, we are soldiers. Let's move.'

The corps members responded and proceeded to the armoury.

Papa Kenny quickly gathered all the other fellowship coordinators in the lodge.

'Please, I want to know how many of our people are still out there. We need to call them to know what the situation is where they are, so we can plan a rescue.'

The fellowship heads had barely answered when they heard noise from outside the lodge. The mob was approaching. Each person grabbed his weapon and was in position. The CLO was there giving orders, 'Hold your fire. Let them get into range before you shoot. Remember every bullet must count!'

The corps members waited for the command. 'Fire!'

They unleashed a rain of lead on their assailants.

A group of corps members ran into Safety of God Church. The pastor took them in and offered them drinks. They declined, because fear had robbed them of their appetite.

'Let us pray,' the pastor charged. 'Quietly' he added.

Everyone took different positions as they communed with God. 'Father, deliver us... Put an end to this violence... Shakaka rontombolo, shekeke keke ma ma ma ma...'

They prayed for deliverance, their voices just above a whisper in holy defiance against their fears and assailants. All of them were lost in prayer, and by the time they realized the church was surrounded; it was too late.

Osato had been running for a while, trying to escape another angry mob. He'd outrun one set when the muezzin called the faithful for prayers. He had not been able to make it to the lodge, so he'd run for the local government. Now, another mob was hot on his heels. Though he had been a long-distance runner in his university days, he had run for long and was getting tired. He decided to run into the church.

The people chasing Osato were getting tired; they knew they could not catch up and he would escape. So, they decided on another way to bring him down. Somebody produced a bow and arrows, and shot. There was a twang, followed by a silent whiz, as the poisoned arrow sailed through the air. Osato was at the door of the church; his face brightened when he saw some corps members inside. As he started to knock, an arrow struck him at the back. He fell to the ground. The poison in the arrow would kill him slowly: it would first render him immobile before he had a brain seizure that would kill him.

The corps members in the church started to shout when they noticed smoke was seeping into the church. The pastor asked them to settle their lives with God. Quietly, they all made their peace with God. As the fire raged some of them sang to God in loud voices and cried; their arms linked. Others tried to make calls. They could not come out because the mob had chained the door from outside. The roof caved in. One of the corps members finally ran out of the church, with fire in her hair. She was hacked down for all her troubles. She died with her eyes fixed on the cross on the pulpit. The church burnt down with the remaining people in it.

'Inyanmiri! Kaffir!' The leaders of the mob said and spat.

III

The CLO and his band of shooters had done a good job keeping the mob away from the lodge. Many of the vandals had died, but it seemed that for every person that fell, two more took his place. Finally, the fear of God had fallen on them and they had taken to their heels. The corps members cheered and maintained their position. Then suddenly a fast moving cloud of arrows sailed towards the lodge.

'Fast, everyone take cover. Those arrows are poisoned; if they so much as graze your skin, you are a goner.'

The corps members hid and tried to get flat metals they could use as shields. Not many could be found. The arrows kept coming; two corps members were hit. A female was hit in the left breast while a male got hit in the foot; his foot was outside the coverage of the metal sheet. The cry that went up was both from pain and anguish at certain death.

The CLO peeped; he saw that the mob was advancing since no

one was shooting at them. They had used the arrows as a smoke screen to advance. The CLO told his men to lay flat and fire at will.

Papa Kenny asked a group to follow him to the roof, and gave some directives. 'The arrows are coming from behind that bush; concentrate fire on that position. These arrows are poisonous; we can't risk getting hit.' The corps members released a volley of bullets. The arrows stopped.

The rest of the assailants were running towards the lodge. The CLO shouted, 'Switch to automatic fire!'

Papa Kenny came down from the roof and went to the room where the fellowship leaders were waiting for him. 'We have a list of those who are not here,' Chika, the kitchen coordinator said.

'Good,' Papa Kenny said. 'Now we need to send them messages or flash them briefly. If they call back, tell them to stay put. If they text back, tell them to give you their location and to stay put; we will come and get them at night.'

'But why don't we call them directly?' asked one of the ladies, with others nodding in agreement.

'Because we don't know where they are.'

'But Papa, is that not what we are trying to find out?'

'Yes, Chika. But if we call them and the phone rings out for long while any of the killers are close, we may compromise their position and put them in harm's way.'

'Okay, I understand now.'

'Alright, please get to it.'

'Papa Kenny!' the CLO called out.

'What's the problem?' Papa Kenny asked.

'You better come and see for yourself!'

They made for the fence in front of the lodge. As Papa Kenny climbed the scaffold, he noticed that those shooting held their fire;

and the females among them had their hands over their mouths. He soon saw why.

There were two corps members kneeling and facing the lodge. The miscreants had machetes to their necks.

'What do we do?' asked the CLO, 'Those are Ekaete and Femi.'

'I don't know,' a confused Papa Kenny replied, 'And we can't use automatic fire so that we don't end up killing them ourselves.'

The CLO did not know what to do either.

'I have an idea,' Papa Kenny said, 'Who are our best shooters?'

'Me, you, Edozie, Nse, Tobi and Saviour'

'Good. All of us are going to aim for the guys around Ekaete and Femi. Hopefully, they will see what we are trying to do and run for it. Then we'll cover them.'

Papa Kenny got one of the guns with a telescopic lens. He shot one of the miscreants dead; as others did same. This caused uproar among the mob.

'Papa, look,' the CLO said.

A machete was going up. As the machete descended, Papa Kenny shot twice. Ekaete and Femi fell down dead.

Everyone on the wall stared at him in unbelief. 'What did you just do?' the CLO asked.

'That was the easy way out for them,' Papa Kenny replied.

'How is shooting our colleagues dead the easy way out!' barked another corps member.

'It's quicker,' he said, and got off the scaffold. 'Shoot the bastards when they are within range.'

The mob couldn't believe what had just happened. They looked from the dead corps members to the lodge. A couple of them charged senselessly towards the lodge, but they were cut down by bullets.

As Papa Kenny shot at mobsters who tried to get into the lodge from the back, he wondered if he had done the right thing in that situation. 'Lord, have mercy on me,' he mouthed.

By seven o' clock that evening, the mob dispersed for prayers. While some corps members kept watch, others went to eat. Papa Kenny and a group went to get the bodies of their fallen colleagues. As they came back into the lodge, a lady ran into Papa Kenny, trying to claw his eyes out. 'Murderer!' she screamed. 'You bastard! You killed my fiancé. Killer. Murderer!'

When they got her off him, she was sobbing quietly; tired of fighting. Papa Kenny had scratches on his face. 'I'm sorry,' he said, his voice heavy with emotion, 'I'm so sorry.'

'Papa Kenny, come and eat,' his assistant called him, after they had sedated the crying lady.

'I'm not hungry. Thanks.' He had a thoughtful look to him.

'Papa, you did what you thought was best,' Yemi consoled.

'Did I?' he asked in a small voice. She was quiet.

'Mama, am I a good person? Am I a good leader?' he asked.

'Yes, without a doubt. If not for you, most of us would be dead. The casualties we've recorded are minimal because of you and CLO's leadership. It was a tough decision and you made it.'

'Thanks,' he replied, with a weak smile.

At 8:30p.m that evening, they called all the corps members they could reach outside the lodge. With their locations known, Papa Kenny split the rescue team into ten groups of four men each. Each man was dressed in a 'danshiki', their weapons concealed underneath.

'We re-converge in two hours. Keep out of sight, and don't use your weapons except it is absolutely necessary. God be with us all.'

They all made for their different rescue areas, armed with their comrades' locations.

Time check: 11:00p.m

Ade and Ochuko heard the thud, as a group made it over the fence. Papa Kenny whistled and Ade replied. The six corps members quickly climbed the fence, along with Halima and Zainab. Whenever they met any Hausa people, they let the fluent Hausa speakers among them do the greeting.

Ade faced Halima, 'Here, take my phone. I'll call you after all this is over.' Halima held unto him and cried, wondering if she would ever see him again.

'I promise to come back to you when things settle down.'

'Please, don't get killed,' she cried.

'I won't.' They shared a kiss, and Ade moved with the others. Halima watched them go in the cover of darkness, one hand on her bosom, and the other over her mouth, 'Asuka lafia' she whispered. It was almost a prayer.

Zainab kissed Ochuko like it was the last time. 'I will see you again, I promise,' he said.

'I know you will,' she replied, smiling while she caressed the side of his face. As he turned to leave, she said, 'Be safe, my love.'

'I will. Thank you for everything.'

'My pleasure,' she said, 'I have to go. Alhaji might have gone to our house to look for me.'

As the six corps members made their way to their lodge, they prayed that other corps members had the same good luck as they did. They were a couple of streets to their lodge and had just turned a corner when they heard painful moans coming from a dark spot, close to a wall, surrounded by shrubs. Two corps members went to find out what was going on.

Ade and Ugochukwu came back with a report. 'Some bastards are raping two female corpers,' a visibly angry Ade blurted out.

'Hey, keep your cool.' David snapped.

'It's attitude like that that will get us all killed,' Papa Kenny said, then added, 'Here is the plan.'

Two new boys joined the group of eight who were taking turns on the girls. One of the new guys said they would like to join in the fun. He spoke in their language, and even had the accent. The original eight didn't mind, while the girls burst into fresh tears. It was the turn of the last of the original eight. As they plunged into their victims, the two new guys pulled out their knives and struck the rapists. Papa Kenny and the three other corps members joined their colleagues and wounded the rapists. The whole thing was fast and the rapists had no chance to shout before they were all knocked unconscious.

Papa Kenny bent over the crying ladies, 'Can you walk?' he asked. They nodded and were helped up. Slowly they all made it back to the lodge.

When Papa Kenny and his group returned to the lodge, they met other groups who had come in. All of them had news of near misses and had seen deaths.

IV

CLO told the group that he heard that the rioters had been given guns and would continue the assault at first light. He asked those who could, to get some sleep. All the men would take turns keeping watch through the night.

'I think we should dig a ditch some metres from the gate.'

'Ah, ahn Pappy K, why?' CLO asked.

'If we dig a relatively deep ditch, it would be easier to kill them as they come at us. The reason is that, when they go into the ditch, they can't aim at us; and climbing out of the ditch, makes them target practice for us. Before they think of getting a plank across, the army should have sent back up,' he said. They went to work.

True to the intelligence they received, the lodge was surrounded by eight o' clock the next morning. The corps members had hardly slept.

'Don't waste your ammo, conserve your bullets. We don't want to run out before the cavalry gets here. Make every bullet count.' advised the CLO. The bombardment began. Bullets whizzed past the corps members and some were hit. The ditch worked. There were a lot of casualties on the enemy's side.

Papa Kenny's mouth opened when he saw an RPG. Before he shouted, he noticed that the person holding the rocket launcher had it turned backwards. The RPG was fired and went into the midst of the vandals. A good number of them died. When the RPG carrier turned it around, he got shot between the eyes.

The CLO finally called the army barracks close by. He was told that soldiers were enroute and would be with them as soon as they could. The soldier told the CLO that he and his people should do everything possible to stay alive. The CLO replied that they would.

Papa Kenny went to see the ladies they rescued the night before. 'How are they holding up?' he asked one of the corps members, who was a doctor.

'They are still in shock. One of them is calm, but the other is not,' replied Dr Tosin.

'It must be the trauma.'

'Yes, you're right.'

'Can I see them?'

'Yes.'

While one slept, the other just stared into oblivion. Papa Kenny sat beside her quietly and prayed.

'Papa, why didn't you let me die?' she asked, not looking at him.

'No one deserves to just die,' Papa Kenny said.

'But I am damaged goods. I have kept my virginity till now. Who would love me now?'

'Jesus loves you, no matter what.'

'Do you love me?' she asked, looking him in the face.

'Of course,' he replied.

'Will you marry me; or let someone you know marry me, after what happened?' she asked, her lips quivering as she stared at him.

He paused. He shouldn't have.

'You see,' she said, 'I want to die!'

'Don't talk like that. No one will know what happened,' he admonished.

'I will; and I can't live with the thought. Kill me or I will take my life.'

Papa Kenny tried to talk her out of her suicidal thoughts, but she asked him to leave. Papa Kenny went to the doctor. 'Put someone with Loveline, she could harm herself if she is left alone.'

'Okay.'

Loveline stabbed herself in the heart before anyone could be assigned to her. No one knew where she got the knife from. Omonigho woke up and saw the bed beside her bare.

'Where is Loveline?' she asked.

No one answered; Omonigho burst into tears. The atmosphere in the makeshift clinic was grave.

The corps members got a call from the Army Barracks. They wanted to find out how the corps members were holding up. The army informed the corps member that they had encountered some difficulties with insurgents in the town. Christians and Non-Hausa Muslims were being attacked. Churches had been burnt; lives and properties had also been lost. Help might be long in coming. The army asked the corps members to hang in there and fight to save their lives by all means.

Papa Kenny got a disturbing phone call from his pastor. A number of his church people were hiding in a cemetery at the other side of town; a few Non-Hausa Muslims were there with them. Papa Kenny saw that what had begun as a political riot had morphed into a religious and ethnic crises.

'Can you and your men come to help us?' asked the pastor.

'I'll see what can be done,' assured Papa Kenny; then he added, 'How many of you are there?'

There was a short silence before his pastor replied, 'Twenty.'

'Okay sir; keep out of sight till we come. God be with you.'

The line went dead.

It seemed that all the noise of the previous hours petered out. Suddenly, there was less chaos. Papa Kenny and CLO ran to the scaffold to see what was happening. They both saw that the insurgents had turned their backs and were walking away.

CLO and Papa Kenny were stunned. The other corps members were surprised as well, but they were alert. Something could be wrong. After about one hour when nothing happened, the corps members decided to venture out. They took two buses and decided to drive into town and hopefully to the army barracks to get help.

The corps members were alert, as the bus rolled into town. Their mouths hung open as they observed the damage. In the heart of the town, a handful of corps members got down from the buses and moved slowly beside the buses; with their guns at the ready. The buses had a number of broken windows; corps members with guns manned the windows.

Papa Kenny didn't like the ease with which they made it into town. He looked to the CLO beside him and shook his head.

'This is too easy,' the CLO said.

'I am thinking the same thing,' Papa Kenny said.

Just then, there was a sound and blood splattered on the dashboard. One of their drivers had been shot. The CLO got in the driver's seat, driving as fast as the cluttered roads would allow; the corps members on the ground ran beside the bus.

The rioters came at them from a side road. Papa Kenny shouted to the corps members to shoot at will and they did. The rioters died in droves while some of them beat a fast retreat.

Quickly, Papa Kenny and two other corps members came down from the bus and picked all the guns, explosives and ammunition they could gather. The CLO moved the bus at a much faster rate. As they drove on, they saw some people come towards them with their hands held high in surrender. They were victims; Christians and Muslims.

'Get them on the bus.' Papa Kenny said.

Suddenly, the bus behind Papa Kenny's bus lurched to a stop. The driver had been taken out by a sniper. The dead corps member was pulled off the steering wheel, and the bus started moving again.

Another shot.

Another shot.

The sniper had started to target Papa Kenny's bus. Papa Kenny knew that if the sniper could stop the bus from moving, every other person on the second bus was doomed.

'We need to locate that sniper and take him out,' Papa Kenny said already opening the door.

The CLO looked at Papa Kenny. 'Don't do it Pappy.'

Papa Kenny looked at the CLO. 'That's the only way. Get where the sniper is; and take him out.' He ran across the street with his weapon.

'Wait!' yelled the CLO, as Papa Kenny ran across the street, 'Damn it!'

'Shit!' Ade said.

Papa Kenny made it across with no shots fired. He lay flat beside a building. He looked round and his eyes fell on a mosque beside where he lay. If he was a sniper, he would hide in the minaret. He made it into the mosque and began to climb the stairs cautiously. He could see the back of the sniper. He raised his gun.

Ade had seen his comrade go into the mosque. 'He needs back up,' he charged.

'Stay put; that's an order!' the CLO replied.

'Fuck you; you are not the boss of me. I can't just sit down and let him die.'

Ade ran into the streets; a shot rang out. Everyone saw how the bullet hit him and how the blood splashed from his head. Everyone saw that he continued running until he fell close to the mosque's entrance.

Just then, two shots rang out inside one of the mosque's minarets. Everyone in the bus waited with bated breath. They did not think of their own safety. Some of the ladies started to sob. CLO didn't know what to say and said nothing. He was about to kick the bus when Papa Kenny came out of the mosque, two arms raised in a sign of victory. Thank God, one of the girls in the bus said, sighing.

As Papa Kenny ran back to the bus, he stopped dead in his tracks. His breathing became laboured when he saw Ade's lifeless body sprawled in the middle of the street. The others joined him beside the body; they positioned themselves to have a three-sixty view and their guns were ready for any assault.

They fought their way to the cemetery, picking more people on the way, and getting another bus. They got to the cemetery a few minutes past four. Close to the city centre, the corps members found that they could not proceed. They were turned back by policemen who told them that staying at their lodge was safer than crossing into the city centre. The police men assured them that their part of town was secure. Papa Kenny and CLO tried to explain that they were corps members and were trying to get to the barracks. The policemen told them again to turn back. That anything beyond the place where they were standing was a death zone. The corps members turned back and rolled towards their lodge to treat their wounded.

Papa Kenny was determined they cover a good distance before the mob re-grouped. When they got close to the lodge, they met an angry looking mob waiting for them.

'What do we do?' Papa Kenny asked.

'I won't stop driving and you mustn't stop shooting.' CLO replied.

Papa Kenny called those in the other buses and told them not to stop, and to shoot as if their lives depended on it.

Eventually, the first two buses rolled into the lodge but there was no space for the third. So those in it quickly disembarked. As the last few persons on the bus struggled to get off, an RPG hit. The bus exploded, a whole family burnt with it.

By seven o' clock that evening, it was evident their ammunition would not last for much longer.

'Our ammo is running out,' CLO told Papa Kenny.

'What?'

'Yes, we need backup; and we need it now.'

Papa Kenny bowed his head to think when they heard some noise coming from inside the lodge.

'You stupid bitch!' It was a corps member with bloodshot eyes called Nnamdi. 'Bitch,' Nnamdi said again, slapping a female corps member. It was Hauwa. Hauwa staggered backwards; a question and shock on her face.

'It's all your fault. Your stupid people have killed us and raped our girls,' Nnamdi yelled.

Hauwa was stunned. 'Nnamdi, please. You can't blame me for what some people are…'

'Shut up!' Nnamdi shouted. 'Show me one Hausa corper who has been raped today. You think we don't know? All those long calls in your language? You people were informed and told to stay safe? To say salaam salaam, when somebody asked for your names? We know. This was the same thing that happened during the civil war.'

A crowd had gathered. But the crowd was divided. Some of them were speaking for Hauwa, while others were speaking against. Nnamdi was enraged. He lunged at Hauwa. 'Bitch, I will teach you to rape our girls.' He dragged Hauwa whose resistance was nothing in the face of his rage. She begged, she pleaded but everyone was too busy arguing with the next person to help her. Nnamdi dragged Hauwa into a room. He was about to shut the door when Papa Kenny raised a pistol to his face; the CLO was trying to calm those arguing.

'Step out of the room,' Papa Kenny said.

'What?' Nnamdi said.

'I said, step the fuck out of the room.'

'This is my room.'

'Hauwa,' Papa Kenny said, 'come out.'

Nnamdi made to say something and block the door.

Papa Kenny pulled the safety clip off the gun. 'Not a word. So, because we have this crisis, you want to add your piece of trouble.'

'Will you shoot me like you did Ekaete and Femi?' Nnamdi asked, in spite.

Papa Kenny said nothing. Hauwa stepped out of the room and Papa Kenny locked Nnamdi in.

Meanwhile, a full scale war of words was going on. The Igbo corps members had turned on the Yorubas, and the few Hausa corps members had found themselves in the middle. The Igbos said the Yorubas could not be trusted. The Yorubas called the Igbos 'cannibals'. The Hausas called the Igbos 'Inyanmiri'. The CLO tried to restore peace.

When the arguing stopped, Papa Kenny and CLO went to Nnamdi's room.

'What was that?' Papa Kenny asked.

'She was laughing over the phone when anytime from now, we could all be killed!' Nnamdi said. 'She was speaking in that their stupid language and laughing.'

CLO stormed out. He came back with Hauwa. 'Is it true what Nnamdi says? That you were laughing on the phone?'

'I was speaking to my parents. I was laughing to put their mind at ease. I never meant any harm; I am so sorry,' Hauwa said.

It was morning; Papa Kenny asked the CLO, 'Has the army said anything again?'

'Just that we should hold out, and that they will be with us as soon as it's possible,' the CLO said, in a defeated tone.

'Hey, we'll survive this. God is with us. The army will come; I know it,' Papa Kenny encouraged.

The CLO stared past Papa Kenny wide eyed. Papa Kenny turned. He saw a crowd, led by five men coming towards the lodge. He and the men with him turned, shooting immediately. Others joined, but they could have well been shooting at rocks.

'Seize fire! Seize fire!' yelled Papa Kenny. They watched as the mob advanced. Papa Kenny was breathing heavily, his hand running over his head. He was confused and scared.

'Papa, CLO, what do we do?' asked some corps members.

'Let me think,' Papa Kenny said. 'We need to save our ammo. These guys have charms and our bullets are useless against their charms. We could as well be pelting them with stones,' Papa Kenny said, and stopped deep in thought, 'With stones!' he repeated to himself.

'Papa has gone mad,' offered a corps member when he saw his leader fill the barrel of a local rifle with sand and stones.

Papa Kenny didn't hear anything; he aimed and said quietly, 'Teach my fingers to battle and my hands to war.' He shot at the approaching mob. His target was the 'untouchable' five.

The 'untouchables' fell down one after the other. 'Fire!' yelled Papa Kenny. The corps members shot at the assailants; a lot of them fell dead, while the others retreated. Papa Kenny's unconventional tactic was based on events that happened amongst cultists while he was back in school.

'CLO, Mike, Ubong, Ahmed, Onome let's go get the weapons they left behind; on me!' yelled Papa Kenny over the noise, and then added, 'Cover us!'

The mob had regrouped and most of the corps members were down to their last clip.

'Conserve your ammo! Seize fire!' yelled Papa Kenny.

The mob was approaching.

'The Lord is my shepherd…' Papa Kenny started, and everyone joined in.

Their praying was cut short when they heard a staccato of gunfire. The rioting mob was cut off from behind. The men of the Nigerian Army, 73 Battalion had arrived and saved the day.

As they drove out of the lodge with the soldiers serving as escorts, the corps members rode in silence; the events of the past days playing in their minds. They were all exhausted. Papa Kenny rode in the NCCF bus which was close to the rear of the entourage. When he looked out at a side road, he saw a lone shooter with an RPG aimed at them.

'RPG!' he shouted.

Boom!

V

Pappy Kenny woke suddenly from a long sleep. The boom from the RPG in his dream was still echoing in his ears. Suddenly, he realized it was the door. Somebody was knocking on his door. Why were they hitting it so?

He opened the door. Ochuko, Ade and CLO were there.

'Haba Pappy, we have been knocking since,' CLO said, smiling and looking into the room.

'I'm sorry. I've been asleep.'

'Haba, Papa, abi babe dey inside?'

'Abeg; no be una two dey follow Halima and Zainab up and down?'

The guys laughed.

'Anyway, Pappy,' CLO said. 'Election posting came out o, and they said we must all report to the local government for transportation first thing tomorrow. But you have to go and check your name first.'

'Oya, Pappy, dress up let's go so that we can quickly come back,' Ade said.

Papa Kenny thought about his dream and shook his head. 'Guys, I no dey go.'

'You nor go?' Ochuko said.

'No' Papa Kenny answered.

'Ah, ahn, after all the wahala wey we don do? Wetin happen?'

Papa told them he had a bad feeling about the election.

The guys looked at one another and started laughing. Ochuko said, 'Yoruba people and fear? Na wa.'

All the guys laughed.

'Pappy, we are going. I will check for you. I know you will change your mind,' CLO said.

Papa Kenny watched them go. He knew what he would do. He would ask the corps member to pray about the election this night. Then, he would tell them that he wasn't going because God revealed to him that it would be chaotic. He decided not to tell them the dream. If he did, he would have to say he killed Femi and Ekaete, or that Loveline and Omonigho were raped by eight boys. First thing tomorrow, he would leave for Lagos and wait the election out.

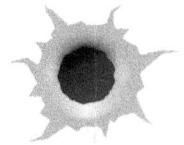

COMING HOME

I

Halima sat up. Her heart was racing, and she was sweating profusely. She had a nightmare: the same one she'd been having since she returned. Her father was beside her in an instant. His presence was comforting and reassuring. 'I am here, my child,' he said. 'You are home now.' He rocked her and asked her to sleep after drinking some water.

Halima's father slept close to her every night. His ear, attentive to her slightest move; his presence, serving as a solid comfort against her recurring nightmares. He had already lost Halima's mother during the time of her absence; he was determined that he would not lose his daughter again.

Halima was happy to be back with the other girls. But she wasn't sure she would ever fit in? How does one fit in after being kidnapped by Boko-Haram and held in captivity for two years? How does one blend, knowing that some of one's friends were still in captivity, suffering the same hell from which she had escaped? She thought about the other girls who had come back, how were they faring? How would they all settle back into Chibok?

Halima sat with her therapist, a nice woman who was assigned to her by the army, by the directive of The Presidency. Her previous therapist was changed because being in a room alone with a man brought back unpleasant memories. Though Halima would herself admit, not all her memories about men were bad.

She lay supine on the couch as her session with the therapist began. Her mind went to the other girls; she wondered how they were faring with their therapists. She knew for a fact that she and all the other girls were scarred for life and that no promise from the government or assistance from well-meaning people could change that. They were grateful for the Nigerians who prayed and the NGOs who demonstrated and believed they would return. But they, the returnees, were the ones who had to live this narrative of return; to decipher if the look on the faces of people who interacted with them was of pity, of scorn or of judgement.

Halima faced her therapist and said, 'Today, I would like to talk about Kashim.'

Dr Sunmisola looked up from her pad and said, 'I would like to hear about Kashim, Halima.'

'I remember my early days in captivity. There were no amenities, no hygiene, no sanitary pads, no privacy and no food. We went without food for days at a time. Because of the lack of hygiene, we knew we would soon start falling sick. But that was the least of our worries: we were soon to be given to some of the men who fancied us.

'Many of the men showed a preference for me. But I was 'lucky' because I caught the eye of Hamza, one of Shekau's top lieutenants. I would not be given to anyone. Hamza had picked me and I was to be his woman. I did not fare better than any of the other girls. Hamza raped me every night, leaving me weak, battered and with new bruises. It was on one of such nights that I met Kashim.

'Kashim is handsome; I think he is about my age. One night, after Hamza had raped me; he went out to clean himself. I lay there bloodied, with semen smeared all over my privates. I could not even stand or walk; yet, I knew Hamza would kick me out the minute he came back. I took deep breaths to gain strength, but they were no good. So, I lay there waiting to be kicked and thrown out. I closed my eyes. 'Why did God allow this? Could He see what was happening to the other girls and me? Did He even care? Did the people of Nigeria care about us? What was the government doing?' I asked these questions as I heard footsteps coming towards the tent.

'I felt a hand raise me gently and carry me out of the tent. I kept my eyes closed as the hand lay me down and cleaned me up. It was then I heard a voice, a boy's voice, singing. His voice was soothing, and the pain was not so bad anymore. But it was dark, and I could not see his face; plus, my face was all swollen. That night, the voice or its owner watched over me, soothing me as I woke up from my nightmares. But by the time I woke up in the morning, he was gone. I did not know him, so I could not find him.

'We were moved across the Nigerian border. As we crossed, I wondered if I would ever come back. Though our abductors often spoke angrily about the military bombing them, it was clear that they still had the upper hand. By the time we crossed the border, a good number of the other girls were already showing signs of pregnancy. My friends and I often held hands and tried to encourage one another. Whenever we talked of rescue and seeing our families again, we spoke in hushed tones. We spoke without believing, but we spoke of it all the same. Talk of rescue became some fantasy that we escaped into to numb the pain of our reality.

'On the other side of the border, food was in short supply. So, the men ate first, followed by the pregnant while the rest of us struggled for scraps. One time, I did not have a meal in four days. I was weak, but I knew that this would not stop Hamza from forcing himself on me that night. He had just come back from a mission and he was in a good mood. The general banter indicated that they had caught an Airforce man and beheaded him for the world to see. That day, I prayed that night would not fall, but it fell with clockwork regularity.

'As I rested against a tree, I heard a whistle. I looked into the bushes but saw no one. Rather a small package sailed towards me with the words, 'Something for you to eat. Eat it fast.' I knew the voice; it was the singing voice. The voice I had made myself believe belonged to an angel. But why didn't this angel show himself? I shared the food with my friends. It was small, but it was food nonetheless.

'That night, Hamza came in drunk. He was not alone. He laughed as he undid his trousers. His uncircumcised penis stared me in the face as did five others. I was about to be gang raped. Hamza took me first. My angel had given me a lube and it helped. I screamed less and was scarred less. But Hamza also cared less. To him, the fact that I screamed less meant that his strength was waning, so he wasn't gentle. He asked the other men to take their turns, but not in his tent. So they carried me outside into the woods, and lay me on the forest floor. They were all drunk and incoherent. I closed my eyes and waited, but no one touched me. After a while, I opened my eyes and saw all five men sprawled on the forest floor. At first, I feared they were dead, but I saw a figure lean over one to check his pulse. My angel had finally shown himself.

'I held him from behind, my naked body clinging to him. Thank you, I said.

He stood there not uttering a word. He turned slowly to face me and slowly took off his oversized shirt. My hands went to my lips as I shook my head pleading with him, 'No, no, no, please! Dan Allah!' He came closer and wrapped his arms around me. I froze, but he was not deterred. He lifted me and took me to a secure place where he put his shirt over me. I kept staring at this boy who was not interested in my body, but my well-being. He looked me over and then made to leave.

'Wait, please,' I held him, 'What is your name?'

He did not answer. Rather he said, 'I have to take care of those men. Go and sleep with the other girls.'

He disappeared into the night, and I wondered who he was and how he came to be with these despoilers.

'The next morning, the five men all had concussions. They blamed it on the drink. If the situation were different, I might have laughed. But I was concerned with this saviour of mine. Where was he? Maybe he was not part of them, I thought. Maybe I had conjured him up in moments of pain.'

II

Some weeks before, when Halima was still in captivity, the camp came under attack from Nigerian troops. Bullets whizzed without discernment; abductor and abductee fell side by side. Bombs dropped from above, exploding into a mixture of debris, shrapnel and bloodied human parts. Halima saw men, women and girls fall dead. She saw a pregnant girl's bowel split open by shrapnel. She fell, puked, said a prayer and waited for certain death.

A hand grabbed her and led her further into the woods. Her angel had come and herded a lot of girls to safety. They all ran for cover, and when he felt they were safe, he ran back to help more girls. Halima watched this boy run back and forth; not a hint of fear in his eyes. All he had was a rifle. The soldiers had captured some of the men, and the girls could still hear the exchange of gunfire. Halima kept praying that her angel would be safe. She was about to go find him when they heard the shuffle of feet coming towards them. Halima's face lit up as she prepared to say her thanks. But the words died in her throat as she found herself staring at the muzzle of a gun. A soldier peered into their faces and asked them to move. The girls were scared, but they moved, one step at a time, towards freedom.

Out of nowhere, a stick knocked the rifle out of the soldier's hands. Shocked, the soldier looked and saw a boy with a stick and a rifle. The soldier pulled out his knife and threatened to gut the boy. Halima tried to intervene, explaining to the soldier that the boy was the one who helped them. She also tried telling the 'angel' that it was okay; the soldier was there to take them all home. But neither of them listened.

The soldier and the boy grabbed each other and grappled. The boy was incredibly strong and quick. The soldier punched him in the side with a free hand, but the boy would not let go of the soldier's knife hand. Both of them fell, wrestling to the forest floor; the soldier found a stone with which he hit the boy at the side of the head. But the boy did not let go despite his bleeding. The girls were scared and ran in all directions, but Halima waited. The soldier got on top of the boy, his knife hand between them and pointed at his mid-section. The boy groaned as he tried to get away. The soldier heaved and fell on him. Halima screamed. Blood spread in the undergrowth.

Halima heard a chocking sound but did not look. She had seen many die, and she did not want to add another to her memories. She felt a tap and saw the boy stand beside her while the soldier drowned in his own blood. He had punctured a lung. The boy picked the soldier's gun and shot him in the head. Halima cringed.

'It is better that way. Less pain,' he said.

Halima saw him in a different light. He did not let them go. Instead, he led them back to the camp.

They had to move because the JTF had discovered their hideout. The JTF had killed many of the terrorists and rescued some girls. But there were many more left, and Halima was one of them. Halima felt nothing but hate for Kashim, the murderer who she thought was her saviour. Especially went she realised he went on missions with the rest of the men. What did he want? Did he also have a girl, one of her friends, who he raped every night? Or perhaps, he did not have a girl, and he was being nice to her to get between her thighs. Not that she could fight back if he ever made the move.

Girls began to go missing; especially the pregnant ones or those with babies. They would go out with some men and not return. Halima soon figured out that they were being used as suicide bombers. Food was running short, and the terrorists decided to kill two birds with one stone: reduce the number of mouths and produce some mayhem through suicide bombing. Halima was secure. No one would touch her because she was Hamza's woman; except Hamza himself gave her up.

One day, Halima's best friend, Hauwa, was selected. Halima

stood and said they would have to take her too. Hamza was furious and pulled out his gun, but Halima would not budge. The boy, no longer the angel she loved, ran and stood between Halima and the gun, pleading for mercy. It was then she learnt his name was Kashim.

'Kashim, get out of my way!' Hamza warned.

The boy stood and pleaded with 'Baba' for mercy.

Halima was mortified. Her angel was the son of her tormentor-in-chief!

They all rode in a truck, with Halima holding unto her pregnant friend's hand. When they got close to a Central Market, Halima was held back while her friend and others were ordered to go. Under their hijabs were explosive vests. They walked towards the market gate, manned by the civilian JTF. They were all being searched. Halima watched as the first girl, on realising she would be discovered, detonated her bomb. Halima saw her friend begin to run, but she was gunned down by some soldiers. Kashim covered Halima's mouth to suppress her scream. She bit into his hand, but he did not let go. The men who brought them drove off, pleased that there were at least some casualties. The news would report it soon.

That night, Halima refused to eat despite Kashim's plea. Hamza did not know and could not care less, so long as he sated his desire. Halima led Kashim to the forest that night and stripped naked.

'I want you to fuck me!' she said.

Kashim looked away and told her to get dressed.

'You can kill a soldier, but you can't fuck me?'

'Get dressed,' Kashim said.

'Then what do you want? Why are you kind to me? Oh, you don't want your father's left over?'

'Get dressed,' Kashim said again.

She started to hit him. She hit him repeatedly and tried to get his trouser undone. He pushed her away and told her to get dressed. She fell to the forest floor and began to cry. Kashim sighed and sat beside her. He covered her with her clothes and leaned her head against him. They sat there under the moonlight; no words were said. No words were needed.

III

Halima went home from her session feeling drained and somewhat lighter. She wondered about Kashim and the other girls still held captive. Were they alive? Were they well? She knew that those of them, who had been released, owing to some secret deal between the government and the terrorists, were not really free. Everywhere they went; people stared at them and treated them differently. She wasn't sure what those people felt: pity, fear, revulsion or awe? It was like walking on egg shells. And Halima knew that not all the girls were taking it well.

Halima was afraid they would all become unfeeling. That they would see and hear of deaths and show no emotion. All the girls tried to deal with their pain in different ways. For some, they became withdrawn, others found different outlets. Halima had constant nightmares in which her thighs were prised apart, and a grenade was stuffed in. She always woke up just before the grenade went off. She knew of some girls whose outlet was sex. They liked it rough and painful. Two of them had raped a boy some weeks back, and she had heard that they were planning an orgy soon. One of the girls had even tried to sleep with her counsellor on her first day of counselling. Halima felt no judgement; she understood. Hadn't she sought tenderness in the unlikeliest of places? What the girls sought was love, but they did not even know how to receive it anymore.

The girls had lost their faith; they needed guidance. When they first returned, some of the girls were made to attend prayer vigils and deliverance sessions, but it hadn't helped. How does pain become exorcised? What balm can heal a broken psyche? Is anguish an evil spirit?

The President had made promises to the nation to look into the psychological and educational well-being of the girls. He had their future in mind, he said. Halima was not sure if that would be enough. She sighed and went into the shelter. In the common room, the TV was turned to the news. Her heart stopped as she saw Kashim paraded among some terrorists who had been captured after an attack on an army base. She screamed.

Halima insisted that she wanted to see Kashim. And because she and the returnees had the ears of the Presidency, her request got to the vice-president. Her request was granted, and she was allowed to see him under close scrutiny. They sat across each other in a make shift interrogation room. Two soldiers stood not too far away, their guns at the ready. The room was bugged, and the military hoped that Kashim would say something that would lead to the freedom of the other girls. Halima thanked Kashim for his kindness during her time in captivity. After that, they simply reminisced. When Halima asked after her friends, Kashim simply nodded and looked away.

'Doctor, let me tell you more about Kashim,' Halima said, during her next session.

'Go on, please,' Doctor Sunmisola said.

'I became pregnant by Hamza, but the baby could not endure my malnourished body. I was sad, Doctor. And Kashim was the one who comforted me in those dark days. Even at my most vulnerable state, he refused to take advantage. He was the one who stood up to Hamza when he kicked me in his tent for losing his baby. Hamza pulled a gun on him, but Kashim stood his ground despite my plea that he should leave. Both men stared into each other's eyes, and Hamza lowered the gun. Kashim led me out of Hamza's tent and said over his shoulder, "I will take care of her from now on, father."

'It was Kashim who made sure that I was among the girls who were to be released. I begged him to come with me, but he refused. He told me that his place was by his father's side. I threatened that I would not go, but he merely smiled. I woke as the exchange was being made. He had drugged me.'

Halima stared into Kashim's eyes and saw the kindness still in them. He looked weak: she could sense fear under his facade of strength.

'I will get you out of here,' Halima said.

Kashim looked into her eyes and smiled, 'Forget about me, Halima.'

'No!' Halima said, 'Many of us girls owe our lives to you; especially me!'

Kashim knew that look; it was one of defiance. It was one that told him that she was bent on having her way. He chuckled as he realised that that was the reason he had drugged her for the exchange. He sighed and nodded. Halima rose to her feet and they took Kashim away. She pushed past the soldiers and gave him a hug. With his hands cuffed, he could only rest his chin on her neck. She shook with fear. As she let go of him, she faced the soldiers, 'He is a good man. Please treat him well.'

IV

Halima spoke to her village head who spoke to the directors of the Chibok programme. Halima secured an audience with the Vice President and pleaded Kashim's case. The Vice President listened and told her Kashim could not be released yet. They needed him to help them get to the leader of the group, and secure the release of the other girls before he could be rehabilitated. Halima spoke to Kashim, but he refused. She kept pleading his case and even got some of the other girls to talk about Kashim's help during their captivity.

The President granted Kashim a pardon. But on the day his pardon was granted, an army base was attacked and some soldiers died; some were missing. The army was ashamed and angry; and wanted revenge. The news that one of the terrorists in detention had been pardoned did not sit well with them.

Halima walked into the base, a spring in her step. She was there to take Kashim home. As she walked into the Commander's office, she saw he had a gloomy look. Her heart began to race, what had they done to her Kashim? Was he alright?

'I am sorry, but Kashim and some other terrorists tried to escape yesterday night and we had no choice but to engage...' the Colonel began.

Halima heard no more, she rose and walked slowly out of the room, the wind pushing her on her way. She could not process it. Why would Kashim decide to escape after he had been pardoned?

As she walked towards the gate, she saw soldiers digging a mass grave beside a pile of bodies. She ran towards the soldiers and pleaded with them to give her Kashim's body. The soldiers refused, but they granted her permission to see the body. The body was riddled with holes and they had not even cleaned him up before putting him in a body bag.

As Halima drove out of the barracks in the company of her village chief and father, she saw a man being asked to run and escape. She saw that the man was scared and refused to move. She saw that the man was pushed, and shots were fired into the sky. She saw that the man was scared and began to run. She saw the soldiers giggle among themselves as the man gained some distance. She saw a soldier aim; she jolted as he pulled the trigger. She saw the man fall forward. She saw the man die.